SIRAAJ
An Arab Tale

*For Physics
in friendship
and good will

Barri Moman

December 2007*

Modern Middle East Literatures in Translation Series

SIRAAJ
An Arab Tale

RADWA ASHOUR

Translated from the Arabic and Introduced by
Barbara Romaine

Center for
Middle Eastern Studies
THE UNIVERSITY OF TEXAS AT AUSTIN

COVER PHOTOGRAPH: CHRIS ROSE
COVER DESIGN: KATHY PHAN
SERIES EDITOR: WENDY E. MOORE

Library of Congress Control Number: 2007936778

ISBN: 978-0-292-71752-7

This translation of *Siraaj: An Arab Tale* is lovingly dedicated to my cousin, Susan Van Haitsma, in recognition of her tireless social activism and the quiet courage with which she lives her convictions.

Table of Contents
ഇ൦൭

Acknowledgments
ഓരു

'Alf shukr—a thousand thanks:

First and foremost, to Radwa, for being inspirational, supportive, and always warm;

To my friend and colleague Bill Granara, who put me in touch with Radwa in the first place;

To the Center for Middle Eastern Studies at the University of Texas at Austin, and in particular: to Jeanette Herman, who first advocated for the manuscript, for giving me the wonderful opportunity of working with the Center; and to Wendy Moore, who took over the copyediting, for unfailing patience and good humor;

To all those who, as the English version of *Siraaj* was taking shape, helped me resolve the questions and occasional riddles that the process of translation inevitably throws in one's path;

And last but not least, to my husband, Najib, and my son, Yusuf, for encouraging me, looking after me, and generally putting up with the inconveniences that my work too often imposes on them.

This translation is, as much as anything, a gift from everyone mentioned here.

Introduction
ၿၥၩ

If framed as a variation on the motif whereby an oppressed people struggles desperately against a brutal tyrant—a theme enacted in real life upon various world stages with lamentable frequency—Radwa Ashour's novel *Siraaj: An Arab Tale* is a familiar story, deceptive in its apparent simplicity. Its uniqueness derives in part from its depiction of the Africans who are so central to the narrative; implicit in this portrayal is an acknowledgment, rare in Arabic literature, of the practice of slavery within Arab societies. Very few modern Arabic works take up the theme of African slavery or connect Africans and Arabs as *Siraaj* does. The immediate historical model for the setting of the novel is nineteenth-century Zanzibar, which was ruled by an Arab dynasty (ancestors of the present rulers of Oman), whose working population consisted of African plantation slaves and poor Arab fishermen. Arresting in itself as a feature of this modern Arab novel, the theme of slavery here also serves a particular purpose, inviting us, the readers, to interrogate the notion of bondage, and find a meaningful difference—if we can—between outright enslavement and life as a supposedly free agent under authoritarian rule.

Siraaj, originally published in Arabic in 1992, is an allegory of contemporary political realities, drawing on the conventions of traditional Arabic storytelling, and the poetry and cultural nuances of those styles. The novel tells the story of two late-nineteenth-century thwarted rebellions: a fictional uprising on an imagined island in the Indian Ocean, and Ahmed Orabi's historic—albeit ultimately unsuccessful—revolt against the khedive of Egypt. Orabi's revolt began in 1881 with a demand for constitutional reform, but collapsed in 1882 with the invasion of Egypt by the British, who opposed the Egyptian nationalist movement that Orabi and his followers represented. The setting of the main plot is the aforementioned island, located in imagination off the east coast of Africa, with an Arab sultan who rules over a population consisting of Arab laboring poor and enslaved Africans. The subplot concerning the character Saïd and his journey is told in the context of the bombardment of Alexandria in 1882, culminating in Orabi's defeat and the British occupation of Egypt.

Much of *Siraaj*'s subtlety is in the secondary strands of the tale, or its subplots: Saïd's journey to Egypt at what turns out to be a crisis in the history of that country, for example, and Tawaddud's fascination with narrative, along with her passionate craving for the written word—the literate world from which she is excluded by her own lack of formal education. The importance of stories, in particular of allegorical or historical narratives, is fundamental to Ashour's sense of cultural survival. This is quite natural in a writer, but especially true for those who have borne witness to the ways in which a ruthless attempt to obliterate a society's essential narratives can be, short of actual genocide, one of the most annihilating features of an assault upon a people.

Some excerpts from Radwa Ashour's essay "Eyewitness, Scribe, and Storyteller: My Experience as a Novelist," published in the Spring 2000 issue of *The Massachusetts Review*, will provide an insight into the way in which she conceived and spun out the tale of *Siraaj*. She refers to modern Arab novelists' alertness to time and place, and their need to bear witness—to record—as common characteristics among contemporary Arab literati. She casts light upon what drives her as a novelist and storyteller not only in the particular time and space that she occupies, but also in the context of storytelling—particularly storytelling that is also witness-bearing—as a human occupation, with complex motivations and underpinnings. Ashour observes that she writes partly as the only means she has "to conceptualize my existence and reconstruct it into meaningful categories";[1] "meaning," she points out, is often elusive, but she hopes that greater lucidity is attainable through the process of writing, that things may begin to "make sense, become a little less unintelligible."[2] More significantly, the creation of a fictional landscape reflecting history and present reality constitutes for Ashour the "reappropriation of a threatened geography and a threatening history [as well as] a retrieval of a human will negated."[3] She elaborates:

> I am inclined to think that the need to record, for the writers of my generation, was also a response to a growing awareness of the constant threat of word manipulation, what I would call ultra-modern

germ warfare tactics. What we lived through and witnessed was denied and disfigured. Our collective memory was subjected to a double pressure, it was attacked from within and from without, with the kind of political language which Orwell once described as, "designed to make lies sound truthful and murder respectable, and to give an appearance of solidity to pure wind."[4]

In *The Book of Laughter and Forgetting*, the Czech writer Milan Kundera, recalling the fall of Prague during the Soviet invasion of 1968, describes the problem thus: "It is 1971, and Mirek [a character in the novel] says that the struggle of man against power is the struggle of memory against forgetting."[5] In a later passage from the same work, another character elaborates:

> "The first step in liquidating a people," said Hubl, "is to erase its memory. Destroy its books, its culture, its history. Then have somebody write new books, manufacture a new culture, invent a new history. Before long the nation will begin to forget what it is and what it was. The world around it will forget even faster."[6]

The Palestinian poet Mahmoud Darwish posits this notion in the context of the Palestinian-Israeli conflict, as a result of which thousands of Palestinians have been left homeless and stateless. After the founding of Israel in 1948, many newly disenfranchised refugees wound up in camps in Lebanon, and the difficulty of their plight was greatly exacerbated by the Israeli invasion of Lebanon in 1982. Darwish evokes a bleak landscape in which a whole culture is expected to efface itself:

> Why . . . should those whom the waves of forgetfulness have cast upon the shores of Beirut be expected to go against nature? Why should so much amnesia be expected of them? And who can construct for them a new memory with no content other than the broken shadow of a distant life in a shack made of sheet metal?[7]

That the suppression of collective memory and the enforcement of widespread ignorance (through propaganda, impoverishment, sustained violence, or a combination of these) may be stunningly effective tools in the hands of a conqueror or dictator is self-evident. For Ashour, a professor of literature and a citizen of Egypt, where as of 2005 the adult literacy rate was only about sixty percent and the government is a democracy only according to the fiction sustained by those whose interests it serves, the relationship between ignorance and oppression has profound significance. Concerning the role of the Arab novelist in preserving the collective memory, Ashour comments:

> [Naguib] Mahfouz, [Emile] Habibi, [Mohamed] Deeb, [Latifa] Zayyat, [Tahir] Wattar, [Abd al-Rahman] Munif, [Ibrahim] Aslan, and [Bahaa] Taher, to name but a few, have directly or indirectly assumed the role of national recorder, half storyteller, half historian . . . To challenge the dominant discourse . . . to attempt to give history visibility and coherence, to conjure up unaccounted-for, marginalized, and silenced areas of the past and the present, this has been my endeavor.[8]

The Arabic word *rawaa*, meaning "to narrate," also has meanings associated with the drinking of water, and with irrigation. Just as drinking water and irrigating crops are fundamental to existence—to survival—so is the story. At one end of the power hierarchy this is fully appreciated by those who will make every effort to counteract or neutralize the power of narrative. At the other end it is apprehended by those who struggle to maintain their claim on the stories—the histories—that belong to them, and to keep those narratives alive and dynamic. In Arab societies, collective memory as the repository of cultural heritage has always been transmitted orally in part; the oral tradition is, however, concomitant, and to some degree coterminous, with the Arab-Islamic world's long and very rich history of literatures that have evolved over centuries into a striking variety of genres. In recent years, literature for oral performance and transmission has been increasingly restricted to conventional theatrical settings, while literacy has become a prerequisite to empowerment in the developing world, if it is to stand a chance against imperialism and occupation—political, cultural, and otherwise. Thus illiteracy, too, can become a form of privation, a fact of which the underprivileged are not unaware.

The Moroccan writer Mohamed Choukri, who grew up in extreme poverty in an environment dominated by violence and starvation, was illiterate until he became an adult. After years of struggling simply to survive, he found that his determination to gain access to the world of those who could not only tell their stories but also tell them to a wide audience—the intellectual world to which the key, he knew, was literacy—overcame any inhibition he might have felt at the prospect of sitting in a classroom with young schoolchildren. Thus at the age of twenty he became a primary school student, not stopping at merely learning his letters, but going on to achieve literary prominence as the author who produced, among other writings, a memoir of his childhood, *For Bread Alone*. When I think of the fictional Tawaddud and the book she stole out of sheer longing, even though she could not read it, I think also of the real-life Choukri, who overcame staggering obstacles to accomplish what Tawaddud's childhood friend Saïd began during his sojourn in Egypt, but Tawaddud herself never got the chance even to attempt.

In *Siraaj*, the importance of the spoken word is embodied in the character Ammar, the African slave who once served as personal attendant to the sultan of the island-state where the novel is set, and who is also the long-time friend of Amina—the novel's central character—whom he has known since she was a child. Ammar, himself unlettered, carries a wealth of stories in his head with which he has entertained generations of the island's children. Ammar's character testifies—as do other features of the novel—to the richness of oral tradition. At the same time, the association between the written word and empowerment is clear, for as a rebellion takes shape on the island, the written messages carried by its emissaries are of crucial importance to the strategic advancement of the revolutionaries' plan. The fatal flaw in the plan is a function of the islanders' naïveté in the presence of an unknown enemy with whom they could not have had the knowledge or experience to know how to contend: a condition education might have alleviated, which is precisely why, under an authoritarian sultanate, formal schooling has never been an option for most of them.

ৎ৹   ৎ৹   ৎ৹

Radwa Ashour received her doctorate in African-American Literature in 1975 from the University of Massachusetts Amherst, where she wrote a dissertation entitled "The Search for a Black Poetics: A Study of African-American Critical Writings." She would later publish a book in Arabic on the West African novel. Ashour is not unconcerned with the issue of slavery, but in *Siraaj*, the condition of oppression that the Africans have in common with the freeborn Arab subjects of the sultan is far more significant than their status as Africans enslaved by Arabs.

In this novel, the fate of the Arabs who are subject to the sultan's rule merges with that of the Africans bound to the plantations or to the palace. Although the Arabs' situation is nominally better than that of the Africans, in that the Arabs are not technically chattels, the two groups nevertheless labor under the yoke of a common oppressor, and the result is a unified front for resistance. This begs the question: in an actual revolution, if the conjoined forces of two such groups did manage to overthrow a tyrant, how would those two groups organize themselves after the successful conclusion of their coup d'état? Would the fact that the revolution was in effect an indigenous one—setting aside in the present fictitious case the Africans' external origins—result in greater cooperation between the parties in building a new society? Would they continue to believe they held a common cause after the removal of the power against which they struggled as brothers and sisters? What, for example, would have happened in Iraq if Saddam Hussein had been ousted without foreign intervention?

It is part of the function of a novel like *Siraaj* to invoke such questions; it cannot, nor should it necessarily attempt to, answer them. To quote Milan Kundera once more, this time in the context of literature and its function in society:

> The stupidity of people comes from having an answer for everything. The wisdom of the novel comes from having a question for everything... The novelist teaches the reader to comprehend the world as a question. There is wisdom and tolerance in that attitude. In a world built on sacrosanct certainties the novel is dead... In any case, it seems to me that all over the world people nowadays prefer to judge rather than to understand, to answer rather than ask, so that the voice of the novel can hardly be heard over the noisy foolishness of human certainties.[9]

These words of Kundera's, spoken in the course of an interview with Philip Roth in the early 1980s, seem prophetic now, as the cacophony of trumped-up, trumpeted certainties that engulfed dissent and led the United States into war with Iraq in 2003 comes to light as the political maneuver it actually was.

Radwa Ashour's novel is similarly apposite, for all that the original Arabic version was published in 1992. In much of the world tyrants impose an iron-fisted rule, and many of them are propped up, overtly or covertly, by the West. Dictators continue to thrive, as the countries they rule stagnate, or are riven by savage conflicts that drive those who can to flee and those who can't, in some cases, to turn to ever more radical and extremist interpretations of religion, politics, or whatever ideology appears to offer them the voice and the empowerment that they are officially or circumstantially denied.

Notwithstanding the warning implicit in Milan Kundera's observations, wherever books may be written, published, and read, the novelist may still serve as one of the most important exponents of social reality. In Egypt, Radwa Ashour joins her voice to those of her contemporaries—whose number includes Sonallah Ibrahim, Bahaa' Taher, Naguib Mahfouz, Latifa Zayyat, Tahir Wattar, Hoda Barakat, Ghassan Kanafani, and Abd al-Rahman Munif, among others—in calling upon Arabs not only to resist foreign coercion, but also to interrogate themselves, their societies, and in particular their leaders. The means to accomplish this rests in recognizing and respecting their own narratives—their stories—and never allowing them to be silenced, or censored out of existence.

Notes

ℰ⟩⟨ℛ

1. Radwa Ashour, "Eyewitness, Scribe, and Storyteller: My Experience as a Novelist," *The Massachusetts Review*, Spring 2000, p. 88.

2. Ibid.

3. Ibid.

4. Ibid.

5. Milan Kundera, *The Book of Laughter and Forgetting* (Michael Henry Heim, trans.), Penguin Books, 1981, p. 1.

6. Ibid., p. 159.

7. Mahmoud Darwish, *Memory for Forgetfulness* (Ibrahim Muhawi, trans.), University of California Press, 1995, p. 15.

8. Ashour, op. cit., p. 87.

9. Kundera, op. cit., p. 237 (Afterword: transcript of an interview with Philip Roth, in which Kundera's wife, Vera, served as interpreter, and a final translated version was supplied by Peter Kussi).

Translator's Note on Transliteration and Pronunciation
ℰↃᏅ

Each language is distinguished by idioms and words for which there is no exact equivalent in any other language, and Arabic is no exception. In general I have tried to get around the challenge this presents to the translator by employing, where precision is elusive, at least an approximate translation. In a few cases, however, I have found an English rendering of the Arabic to be so awkward as to interfere with the flow of the narrative. In such instances, I have transliterated the Arabic word or expression, and explained it in either the glossary or the endnotes. Generally, Arabic words in this text have been transliterated so as to make them, insofar as possible, phonetically intelligible to the non-Arabic speaker. In some cases—in the proper names Saïd and Ammar, for example—phonemes that do not exist in English have simply been left out. Some words and names do contain the symbol ʿ, which represents a liquid consonant somewhat resembling a retroflex "r."

The name of this novel's central character, Amina, calls for a brief explanation. The correct pronunciation is indicated with perfect precision by the Arabic script, but it is more difficult to convey in Roman characters. The name more or less rhymes with the English word "stamina"; this is significant because pronunciation can affect meaning, and many Arabic names correspond to meaningful words in the standard lexicon of the language. Pronounced correctly, the name given to *Siraaj*'s heroine connotes peaceability and fidelity.

In making decisions relative to transliteration and spelling in the course of translating this work, I have been guided more by my own apprehension of both Arabic and English and their respective phonologies than by any explicitly systematic approach. I hope that the result will be as helpful as possible to all readers, whether conversant or not with the Arabic language.

SIRAAJ
An Arab Tale

CHAPTER ONE

Amina and the Sea
ℰ✕ℛ

Amina is afraid of the sea, but to her heart she pretends otherwise: she gets up before the rooster crows, and begins her day by going down to the beach. She stares through the darkness out to sea and whispers a prayer. After that she makes her way to the port and inquires, "Any news?"

"No news."

She walks along the path that leads to the hill, then begins her ascent to the high house. She passes by the dungeon and hears the murmurs and muffled voices. She continues the climb to the women's quarters, which are wrapped in silence and the crash of the waves.

By the time she reaches the kitchen courtyard, the darkness has faded and the sky has burst into the colors of sunrise. "*Bismillah al-rahman al-rahim,*"[1] she says, as she hauls out the sacks of flour and commences opening them one after another. Then she begins the process of sifting. The other women don't arrive until after Amina has finished kneading the dough and left it to rise. The women flock to their tasks, while the slaves carry in the daily provisions of fresh-killed meat, baskets of fish, and crates of fruits and vegetables.

After the call to afternoon prayer, Amina knots her handkerchief around two loaves of bread—her day's wages—picks up her bundle, and retraces her steps homeward, grains of flour still clinging to her dress and headscarf. Her body gives off mingled odors of the day's sweat and baked bread. She stops by the port.

"Any news?"

"No news."

She proceeds to the beach, sits down facing the sea . . . and waits.

ℰ   ℰ   ℰ

She had been a lisping child not four feet tall when her grandfather took her with him. It was a night when the full moon cast its light

1

on the men and the sea. Mounted on camels, they made their way along the beach, singing. She was afraid, despite the singing, the moonlight, and her grandfather's strong arm encircling her as she rode before him on the camel. The sea was at ebb tide, and they advanced farther and farther into the wet sand, searching for ambergris. She stared at the moon in alarm, then turned and buried her head in her grandfather's shoulder, and began to cry, begging him to take her back to her mother. Did her heart know, then, and speak to her?

Men go to sea, they go and then they come back . . . they go and then they don't come back, so the women go out to wait for them, their shoulders rigid with fear, furrows of anxiety etched in their faces. Amina saw it all: the women striking their cheeks in lamentation, when they knew for certain, rending their garments, wailing with cries that split the air, cleaving it in two as the executioner's blade cleaves the living head from the body.

They say that the sea is generous; even as she fears its treachery, she never admits her fear, but rather dissimulates, even to her own heart.

       ဆာ   ဆာ   ဆာ

Amina awoke and breakfasted on a loaf of bread, three dates, and a draught of water. Then she set out for the high house. As usual, she heard the *muezzin* give the call to dawn prayer as she was climbing the hill, but contrary to the normal routine, she found the manager, Umm Latif, and Tawaddud receiving the daily provisions from the slaves, who had also arrived early. When Amina began opening the sacks of flour, she noticed that there was more than the usual quantity; then she saw the slaves coming with extra meats and baskets and crates. "Is it Thursday?" On that day the women would prepare foods both more plentiful and more enticing, because the Sultan would take a new concubine and it was necessary that the household be submersed in a festive atmosphere and a sense of abundance. But it wasn't Thursday, and what the slaves were bringing in was many times more than the usual quantity, so what could the occasion be?

By daybreak the kitchen courtyard was teeming with women preoccupied with food preparation. Umm Latif announced in her strident voice that the work in the kitchen would go on for two days in a row, because the Sultan was to host a great banquet the following day.

Was the Sultan planning to take another wife besides Lady Alia

Bint al-Mohsen, his lawful wife, who wielded absolute authority in the high house? The Sultan had more than fifty concubines with whom he slept by turns, and God had blessed him with dozens of sons and daughters. Some of them had married and begotten him grandchildren, and some were still infants at the breast. But Lady Alia—by the will of God the most high and powerful—had remained childless, stalking about in her sandals of wood inlaid with gold and jewels, so that hearts trembled with fright and children ran in terror, and none in the high house could breathe freely except when Bint al-Mohsen, bearing lavish gifts and accompanied by her serving women, set out for Yemen to visit her father. But she was never away for more than a month, after which she would return to spread gloom and fear wherever she went in her fancy sandals. An austere and coldhearted woman she was, who never smiled—had the hardness of her heart spread to her entrails, turning them to stony ground in which no seed could take root, or had her heart turned to stone from grief over the absence of offspring? Amina pondered as she stood before the fire flattening the loaves. The absence of children wouldn't harden a tender heart. Ammar used to hide lumps of sugar in his pocket for Saïd—Ammar, cut off like a tree limb, fatherless, motherless, wifeless, and childless, yet for all that, he spread as the branches of jasmine spread over the walls of the houses, telling the children stories that they would then demand from their mothers at bedtime: "We want one of Ammar's stories"—the same stories he had told Amina when she was a child.

"Tell me a story, Ammar . . ."

"The story of the frog who married two wives and took to croaking his complaints all night long, or the story of the box in which the children collected stars?"

"The story of the sun and the moon."

Ammar told her the story, and Amina laughed, clutching the hem of his *jilbaab* to keep him from leaving her.

"I must return to the palace, Amina."

"I'll let you go after you tell me the story of the box of stars."

So he would tell her the story and then go to work.

"The absence of children wouldn't harden a tender heart," murmured Amina as she attended to her baking.

After the dusk prayer, the women stopped working and sat down to eat: a loaf for each and a few dates. One of them asked the manager, "What do you say, Umm Latif, what's the occasion for this banquet?"

Umm Latif dodged the question, though she was bursting with the secret of what the women wanted to know.

"Is the Sultan going to take a new wife?"

Umm Latif leapt to her feet as if Bint al-Mohsen had startled her with an unexpected appearance. Her heavy body shaking with agitation, she shouted a rebuke, "You crazy fool, I'll cut out your tongue if I ever hear you speak like that again! Lady Alia is the daughter of a sultan, and mistress of the island, so how could the Sultan take another wife?"

"So what's the occasion, then?"

"Distinguished guests are to visit the island."

"Is the Sultan of Zanzibar coming to visit us?"

"Is Lady Alia's father coming from Yemen?"

"Has a prince of Oman asked for the hand of one of the Sultan's daughters?"

The women's questions rained down upon Umm Latif as they clustered around her, but she said nothing, only rose heavily to her feet and went to the toilet. She returned with a supercilious, all-knowing smile, and sat down in silence, although her eyes never left the women's faces, as she waited for them to resume their talk. But the women, plainly exhausted, lay down and gave themselves up to fatigue. Then Umm Latif could not bear to wait any longer, and she announced in a voice she tried to keep to a whisper, but which rang like a bell, "Tomorrow the queen of the English is coming to the island."

The women who had lain down but not yet succumbed to sleep got up again, while the others adjusted their positions in order to hear better.

"The English?"

"That's right, the queen of the English!"

"Does a woman rule the English, then?"

"A woman rules them. Such are foreigners: with them everything is upside-down!"

Tawaddud said, smiling mischievously, "Everything is upside-down with them: they wear their sandals like gloves and walk on their hands!"

"Good heavens!" exclaimed a woman in astonishment. Tawaddud laughed.

Umm Latif whispered, as if she was revealing a vital secret, "The queen of the English will come with her husband, but her husband is not the king; he's only the queen's husband."

"There is no god but God!"[2]
"And can the queen buy slaves?"
"Of course she can."
"Is she allowed to sleep with them?"

At this point Umm Latif was brought up short, for the question perplexed her, like a riddle without a solution. She made no reply.

Tawaddud said, "If it were permitted by English law for the queen to sleep with her slaves with impunity, then there would be no doubt that the children were hers—right, Umm Latif?"

Umm Latif kept silent until Amina's question came to her like a lifeline.

"When will the ship arrive, Umm Latif?"

"Tomorrow after the noon prayer—that's what Lady Alia says."

Amina was not concerned with the women's talk, or with the solution to Umm Latif's riddle. Her heart was quivering with hope, for who could tell, perhaps the crew of the queen's ship had seen him, or perhaps he would return with them. Would he return with them? Amina spent a sleepless night, thinking about a ship at anchor from which gazed Saïd's face, like the moon.

In the morning the kitchen courtyard was filled with women already busy with preparations for the banquet. They were mixing rice, spices, raisins, and almonds, stuffing lambs, cleaning and frying fish, and preparing vegetables for stewing. The Sultan's women came to assemble luscious concoctions the secrets of whose preparation none but they knew. The Circassians, the Ethiopians, and the Byzantines—each group withdrew to a corner to prepare dishes with which to dazzle their peers and prove the superiority of their race.

Then Alia Bint al-Mohsen appeared, and walked around the courtyard scrutinizing the work, giving instructions and orders. The Sultan's women were frightened of her, concealing their hatred behind friendly smiles and greetings, while Umm Latif followed her around, out of breath, repeating over and over, "As you wish, my Lady," and "Your wish is my command," and "You command and we obey, oh jewel of the island and saint of its blessing." No sooner had Bint al-Mohsen left the courtyard than Umm Latif rushed to the toilet, where she stayed until it seemed she would take up residence there.

Tawaddud laughed, and leaned toward Amina, whispering, "Bint al-Mohsen is as tall as a palm and Umm Latif follows her around, so short she's hardly any taller even when she stands up! Poor Umm Latif!"

"Tawaddud, will you come with me to ask the English sailors about Saïd?"

"I'll come."

As soon as Amina finished her work, she requested permission from Umm Latif for herself and Tawaddud to leave.

The manager objected, saying that there was "no time and no reason to leave." She made a tour of the courtyard, attending to the work. Then she came back and said, "Go, Amina—perhaps you'll hear good news . . . God is generous. Go with her, Tawaddud."

On their way, Amina and Tawaddud heard the reports of the cannons, which were usually fired only twice a year, on the night of the Lesser Feast and on the night of the Great Feast.[3] Hoping it was a good omen, the two continued on their way down the hill, until they caught sight of the tumultuous crowd and, at the entrance to the port, the men whose job it was to greet important guests by blowing brass horns and beating drums that were suspended from their necks.

Then the queen appeared: a stout woman wearing a gown that left part of her bosom exposed, defined her waist, and—below the waist—spread voluminously in stiff, heavy folds, like a tent set up to accommodate several people. Her delicate features were all but submerged in the round face that seemed to rise directly from her shoulders as if she had no neck. There was a crown on her head, a necklace round her neck, earrings in her ears, rings on her fingers, bracelets on her wrists—all diamonds sparkling and glittering in the noonday sun. The queen proceeded slowly and deliberately; the Sultan walked with her, and beside her massive form he appeared slight and insubstantial. He was wearing a white *jilbaab* and an embroidered *abaya*, with a turban on his head. Following them were white men in uniforms that looked like the attire of navy captains.

The Sultan accompanied his guest to the center of the square, where there was a large model of a scale. The queen climbed into one of the pans. Amina wondered at the customs of the English, who would weigh their queen thus in a public square. She turned to Tawaddud, and whispered in disbelief, "Are they doing that so as to find out how much weight she'll put on in our country?"

Slaves approached the scale and began to fill its other pan with ingots of gold.

Tawaddud exclaimed, "The Sultan wants to honor the queen with a gift of her own weight in gold!"

A man standing near her commented, "But she's so fat that it will be the ruination of him!"

Tawaddud replied with an ironic smile, "Not to mention all the clothes and jewels she's wearing, which must weigh a good many *rotls!*"

"Heavens!" Amina murmured. "Oh, the ways of the wealthy are odd."

The queen got down from the scale and shook hands with the Sultan. The procession moved toward the castle amidst the hubbub of the crowd, the drumbeats, and the blasts of the horns. Tawaddud went to get Hafez to help them find someone who spoke English, to make inquiries with the English sailors. Amina sat down to wait until Tawaddud returned with Hafez and an interpreter, and then they all set off to look for the sailors.

"A fourteen-year-old boy named Saïd, son of Abdullah and Amina. Brown skin, curly hair, green eyes, and an old scar under his right eyebrow. He was wearing a white *jilbaab* and was guarded by an amulet half the size of my palm."

"His name is Saïd, his father is Abdullah the pearl diver, and his mother is Amina the baker."

It grew dark outside as Amina, Tawaddud, and Hafez followed the youth who spoke the language of the English, and who repeated the same words time after time for the ears of the sailors who had come on the queen's ship. They listened, and shook their heads, "No."

CHAPTER TWO

The Cares of the Sultan
𝔰🟢𝔯

As soon as the queen's ship had put to sea, the Sultan turned to go back to the castle, hoping that thereafter the English ship would never again drop anchor on the shores of his island.

When Admiral Seymour, acting as deputy to the government of her highness the queen, had presented him with the request, he had asked for some time to think. He thought of writing to the Sultan of Zanzibar to seek his advice and counsel, but then he decided against it, calculating the risks. What if that fox should take advantage of his uncertainty? He might interpret it as weakness, send in forces, and take over the island. He might collaborate with the English; they might depose him and appoint Bint al-Mohsen as ruler in his place. After all, wasn't her father, in Yemen, the intimate friend of the English, and were they not ruled by a woman?

The English were evil, no doubt about it. For many years he had been convinced of this, for he had sent his son Mohammed to study in their country. He said to him, "Go, Mohammed, and pay close attention to whatever you see and to everything that happens around you. Be my eyes and ears, then come back and tell me about their customs, their laws, their traditions, and the particulars of their lives. Inform me of everything, and look out for yourself, your money, and your religious faith—and don't mix with them except insofar as it may serve your purpose and your mission. Stay away from women, apart from those of your slave girls to whom you are permitted access. Don't eat pork or drink wine, else you'll lose your reason, your thoughts will be erased, and you'll become like those sailors of legend who ate of the sorcerers' food and became like beasts that know not what is done to them: the more they ate, the emptier they grew, while the sorcerers kept feeding them more and more so as to slaughter and devour them."

The Sultan opened a cupboard and took out the box in which he kept his correspondence. From the box he took out Mohammed's letter in order to reread it:

> This country is a curious place with strange laws, and the customs of its people differ in the extreme from ours.
>
> Their queen sits upon the throne and wears a king's crown, but the scepter of authority is not in her hand; rather, it is held by a group of ministers headed by a prime minister and an elected parliament, which discusses affairs of state, issues policy decrees, and pays the queen a predetermined annual salary.
>
> There is in this country agriculture, commerce, and industry. The factories operate day and night, with huge machines the likes of which no eye has ever seen. The machines are run by thousands of trained men, women, and children.
>
> If differences arise between the workers and the factory owners with respect to the workers' concerns, then the workers assemble and go out into the street, where they obstruct traffic and shout their demands, and they may clash with the policemen hired by the government to maintain security.
>
> The women of this country go about unveiled. Some of them stay at home, while others work in the factories, and still others study at institutes of learning. I once saw a crowd of women thronging the streets, demanding equal voting rights with men in the election of the parliament which oversees affairs of state and policy.
>
> Their capital is bigger than our island. Their streets are wide and lit by lamps implanted like trees on either side of the road. Their ports are filled with ships like buildings, their shops piled with goods imported from the ends of the earth, east and west, and their factories stand adjacent to one another in those districts whose skies are painted black with the smoke that billows from their towering chimneys.
>
> And all this, my father the Sultan, is but a tiny part of what I've seen, and of the many things that have astonished me. I shall provide you with more information.

The Sultan reread Mohammed's letter, then folded it and put it back in the place where he kept it.

The English were bearing down hard now, and had been for years. They bore down, exerted their authority, showing mercy not even to their closest friends. For here was the Sultan of Zanzibar suffering their commands, forced to accommodate them even as he beheld the ruination of his country under the conditions they imposed, and he without recourse, helpless as a sparrow in the talons of a hawk.

He had seen with his own eyes how they dictated to his father, Sultan Khalid—God rest him—that he give up the slave trade. Such trade had been all to the good, bringing in a solid cash flow and supplying the slave labor that was the mainstay of the island's agriculture. The ships used to sail to the shores of Africa, raid the more prosperous villages, and return laden with their black gold,[1] which they would sell for a fine price, keeping for themselves the hardiest of the men and women. But the English had insisted, then threatened, until his father—God be pleased with him—had been forced to submit to their will. His father had said, "Thank heavens, my son, that our farms are well supplied with slaves, who will keep having children, by the grace and the permission of God."

Then his noble father had died and that idiot, Aliaddin, had succeeded him. But God had seen fit for him—the present Sultan—to get rid of him, and after that he had consolidated his holdings and established his reign through just and lawful means. What now if the English should come and impose their system on the island, allowing the slaves to gather in the open, announcing their demands, the way the factory workers in the Englishmen's own country did?

The slaves were a wretched lot, and nothing availed with them but the stick and the whip. If they were dealt with leniently, there would be chaos: they would turn the island upside down and set themselves up as its masters. His father—God lighten his earth[2]—had been a perspicuous ruler. "Beware of the slaves, Nuʿmaan," he had said, "for they are half the population of the island, and if they should rise against us, we and all we possess would be lost. Give charitably to them of what is yours, but on no account indulge them, and if some upstart youth among them should be seen making trouble, cast him into the dungeon as an example to the others—don't wait for him to act; break him before he musters the courage to do anything. Thus you will uproot the arrogance from their souls and sow fear in their hearts, ensuring their obedience to your authority. The fishermen, the mariners, the blacksmiths, the carpenters—all these we can manage, for they are fewer in number and more dispersed, the resentment in their hearts not so volatile. Trust no one, my son: beware of all, but be especially wary of the slaves, for it is their nature to be treacherous—they are a filthy lot, who have inherited from Satan the sin of pride, and God has punished them by making them slaves."

His father, God rest him, had abstained from the slave trade, and bound himself by contract, but the English ships that came to investigate and make sure their injunction was obeyed continued to come and go in the region on the pretext of preventing piracy and ensuring the safety and security of commercial activities.

On his accession to power, they had come demanding that he refrain from setting up a base on the island for any other country, and he had agreed. But they wanted a legal document, and how could he refuse, with no power to resist them? The choice was a hard one, both alternatives bitter: if he said no, they would depose him, and if he said yes, they would control him. He gave them the document:

> I, poor servant of God the exalted, Nu'maan bin Khalid, Sultan of the island known as the Jewel of the Arabian Sea,[3] do hereby swear and bind myself neither to enter into any decision or agreement or alliance with another nation without the agreement and consent of the glorious English empire, nor to guarantee or give or sell or mortgage any portion of the island's land to the agents or subjects of a foreign nation.
>
> Further, it is my wish to be under the contract and guardianship of the glorious English empire, bound by her guidance and her oversight, as God is my witness.

He knew as he was signing the document that he was like the fool who opens his door to a stranger and invites him into his home, but there was no recourse open to him . . . nor was it within his power to refuse a termagant to whose will other rulers greater and stronger than he had submitted.

The Sultan went out onto one of the balconies of the castle, and stared down at the shoreline of the island. He felt oppressed, his spirits heavy, as he thought about his threatened wealth: his own riches, this island, its land, its slaves, the pearls in its ocean depths, and the ambergris borne aloft on its waves—his possessions, rightfully inherited, and how was he to preserve them? If he allowed the English to establish their base, they would sweep him away with their army and their commerce, and if he didn't permit this, they would impose their demands by force, perhaps deposing him or perhaps keeping him on as they had kept on his wife's father and the sultans of other tribes in the region of Aden: as a puppet with no will or authority of his own, serving the English in return for a monthly stipend of no more than five hundred *riyals*. Nor were the Germans any better or more generous; turning to them would be jumping out of the frying pan and into the fire. For the Germans would come, and the English would come, they would divide up the island, and it would come to a siege, with him crushed to a powder between the two. It seemed to the Sultan that there was a spear pointed at each of his eyes and that he was compelled to choose on which one of them he was to be impaled.

For a period of eight weeks after this, anxiety rode the Sultan, so much so that he didn't initiate any new women, nor did he sleep with any of his present concubines, until rumors began to spread through the high house, and from there to the rest of the island. Some said that the Sultan was ill, while others said that he was as virile as ever. Whispers went round that one of his enemies had put a spell on him so that he became impotent from nightfall until dawn. All eyes were upon Bint al-Mohsen as she trudged around in her sandals of wood inlaid with gold and jewels, for who else might the culprit be?

Then Admiral Seymour arrived to negotiate on behalf of her majesty the queen and her government, and the Sultan received his delegation with honors, informing him that he would be pleased for the English army to have a base on the island, and that the presence of such a base would be a boon to it, an honor to its people, and a tribute to its ruler.

"We have but one condition. We shall appropriate for you the place you choose, from the island's beaches, and the acreage you require, our only condition being that you not permit your soldiers to leave the base or to fraternize with any of the island's residents."

The admiral replied, "In principle we have no objection, but there are certain practical considerations of which we must take account."

"Such as?"

"Such as the provisioning and servicing of the base."

"These are minor issues, Admiral, my good sir. We shall provide you with grain, meat, fruits, and vegetables, as well as fresh water and a number of slaves for your maintenance.

"These slaves are a gift from me, and they will be part of your own fortune; they will reside with your soldiers at the base and will not leave it or return to mingle with any of the islanders."

The agreement was concluded, and recorded in written documents. Then Admiral Seymour signed it as a representative of her majesty the queen's cabinet, and the Sultan stamped it with the seal of the Sultanate.

CHAPTER THREE
An Account of What Happened to Saïd
ଛୁଠ୍ୟ

Saïd returned to the port and found no ship anchored there. He asked dozens of sailors and porters, crossing the port from end to end several times, until the daylight began to fade, and then the disc of the sun sank behind the sea, the world dimmed, and night advanced.

He sat down, hungry and exhausted, unable to believe that the ship had put to sea without him, or to understand why it had left before its scheduled departure time.

When he would laugh uproariously with his friend Hafez, his mother used to listen anxiously and murmur, "God watch over him." Did she know, then, that excessive pleasures would inevitably be followed by great troubles?

Saïd had never been as happy in his life as on the previous day when he had followed Young Mahmoud in the streets of the city, which seemed to him like a bag of tricks. Young Mahmoud had shown him the steam locomotive that belched smoke and sped along, giving off a whistle like that of a ship; likewise, he had shown him the horse-drawn carriages in the paved streets where their footfall raised no dust. He saw the fortress of Qaitbey, which was grander than the Sultan's castle, and he had seen the palace of the khedive, which was still more grand than both of them. And with his very own eyes he saw the places frequented by people who sat on chairs and ordered drinks, which were brought to them as they sat there like princes. When he returned to the island and described all this to Hafez, he might not believe him, might think he had made up half of what he said from his own imagination.

Young Mahmoud said to him, "You're lucky, man . . . you travel by ship and roam the world, then come home like Sindbad the Sailor[1] and live in a palace, invite your friends, and hold parties and all-night bashes for them!"

"Who is Sindbad the Sailor?"

14

"Haven't you heard of him?"

"No."

"Or of Clever Hasan?"[2]

"Never heard of him."

Incredulous, Mahmoud asked him, "Nor Orabi?"[3]

Then he started to tell him one tale after another: from Clever Hasan facing the she-ghoul who said to him, "Had you not greeted me before you spoke, I'd have eaten your flesh and then your bones!"; to Orabi on his horse in the palace courtyard telling the khedive, "We are not your servants and you are not our master!"; to the foreigner in whose house his brother worked ("He's got a face like the rear end of an ape, and he eats two *rotls* of meat every day!"); to Sindbad who carried an ailing old man on his shoulders, then saw his hooves and realized that it was the devil in disguise.

Saïd walked behind his companion, amazed at his tales, his charm, and his ironic comments. In spite of all Mahmoud's talk of how lucky Saïd was because he roamed the seas, Saïd felt it was Mahmoud who was the lucky one, because he lived in this vast and beautiful city, constructed not just of buildings but of wonders.

He proceeded with Mahmoud from Burg Qaitbey[4] to Burg al-Silsila,[5] and from Alexandria's railway station to its markets thronged with buyers and sellers. When they were overcome with fatigue and pinched with hunger, they sat down to eat bread with delicious hot patties of a mixture fried in oil that Mahmoud bought. Saïd bit into one to taste it, repeating its name to himself with pleasure: falafel. The two boys sat together and ate until they were full. They pledged their friendship. Indeed, Mahmoud had won Saïd's heart, and it was as if he had known him all his life, not merely for the two days since the ship had moored at the port of Alexandria. He wished he could stay longer in the city.

But when he found that the ship had left, Saïd was not so happy about the idea of staying in Alexandria. He was frightened to the point of panic, for there was no place for him to take shelter, nor any work by whose profits he could feed himself; indeed, there was nothing for it but to wait until the following day when he could look for Mahmoud and seek his help. But what if he didn't find him? He was overcome by exhaustion before he found an answer to this question. He sank into sleep, and slept until morning.

The sun was about to set when Mahmoud at last appeared. Saïd nearly burst into tears as he ran toward him, pouring out his story and all that had befallen him.

Mahmoud took him to his home, and Saïd spent the night with Mahmoud's family, who fed him, and asked him about his family and his country. Mahmoud's father said to him, patting him on the shoulder, "They say that the English ships are drawing near to our shores, and that they have evil intentions toward us. It may be that the captain of your ship hastened his departure on hearing of this business. Have no fear and don't worry—you are at home and among family. Tomorrow I'll take you with Mahmoud so that you can work with us as a porter at the railway station. What God chooses is always for the best."

Saïd spent three days with Mahmoud and his family, and those three days nearly erased from his memory what had happened to him. During the day he was occupied with carrying travelers' baggage and other possessions, while in the evening Mahmoud would take him out to stroll around the city. They would talk, laugh, eat *termis* and *chufa*,[6] and they would pass under the window of the girl with whom Mahmoud confessed to Saïd he was in love: "Her face is like the moon . . . and her smile—oh, if you could see her smile, Saïd!" They passed the front of the house, stealing a glance at the window, but luck was not with them.

It seemed to Saïd that God had compensated him for his losses, for he thought no more either of the ship that had left him behind or of his mother who awaited him, until three days had passed and on the fourth he was startled by the sound of an earthshaking crash. The news spread about the station that the English ships were bombarding the forts, then pursuing the bombardment as they advanced by sea, relentlessly and thunderously, so that people began to run for home, cursing the English and calling upon Orabi to break their backs and vanquish them once and for all.

"Are you afraid?" Mahmoud asked him.

"No."

"Come with me, then."

"Where to?"

"To the sea, so we can find out what's going on."

Saïd would have preferred to go back to the house, but he didn't say so to his friend—what if Mahmoud thought he was scared?

They headed toward the shore. A great many folk were going the other way, and they said that the English ships were pounding the city from every direction: Agami, Mex, Qaitbey, al-Silsila, and the East Gate. Saïd and Mahmoud saw for themselves flaming missiles shooting from the direction of the sea toward the forts.

16

"But, Mahmoud, why are the English attacking Egypt?"

"Because they're sons of bitches, first of all!"

"But why?"

Mahmoud didn't answer the question. Saïd saw him leap into the air waving his arms like a lunatic and shouting, "Look, Saïd! Listen, Saïd, the forts are giving it back to them! The English are firing from the sea and the forts are returning fire! The forts are shooting at them the way they're shooting at us! Orabi, he's a real man, folks, Orabi's a real man!"

All at once, Mahmoud began to run. Saïd had no idea what had gotten into his friend, who was running like the wind, without looking back or changing direction. Saïd began to run after him, calling to him, until he ran out of breath, without managing to catch up to him. He stood panting, in despair, and watched until Mahmoud vanished from sight.

Saïd remained there waiting for Mahmoud to come back. When he had waited a long time, he went across the road and crouched down, out of the sun, in the doorway of a building that faced the beach. But why had Mahmoud run off like that so suddenly? Had he gone to join Orabi's men in the fortress of Qaitbey? And why hadn't he said something to him, so that they could go together?

Saïd stayed there, crouched in his place, waiting with his eyes fixed on the road.

The bombardment had stopped and total silence had descended over the place. The road appeared deserted, with no passersby, no horse-drawn carts, no sellers of *termis* or licorice root or roasted corn. When it grew dark, Saïd thought of returning home; perhaps Mahmoud had preceded him there. But what if he hadn't returned? His father and mother would ask Saïd about him, and what would he say to them? Then, too, Mahmoud might come here looking for him, and if he didn't find him, he would judge Saïd a coward who had gone off and left him.

Saïd decided to remain in his place until Mahmoud came back. After a while he grew afraid that he would be overcome by sleep, so he stood up and began pacing back and forth, his gaze fixed on the road, on the lookout for the face of his friend with his eyes full of laughter and his familiar mannerisms. He called to mind Mahmoud's image, willing it to appear, then stared at the street, finding there nothing but the dreary darkness . . . until daybreak, when the bombardment resumed and the roar of the missiles deafened the ears. "Now what's happened?" Saïd wondered, seized all at once by acute panic. He began repeating shrilly to himself, "I must look for Mahmoud, I must look for him!" And he started running in the direction Mahmoud had taken.

When he got close to the fort, he saw many soldiers leaving it, some with their heads bandaged or their arms in plaster, others bearing stretchers upon which wounded men lay. Some were hurrying, while others walked with deliberate steps. All of their faces were pale and ravaged. Saïd tried to ask them about Mahmoud, but they advised him to get away from the place.

"The cannons have been destroyed, the forts wrecked," they told him. "We have raised our white flags, and the English are coming."

"And Mahmoud?"

He found none who would answer his questions, but he did not give up hope. He continued his ascent, until a stern-looking man with a thick white mustache blocked his path. The man was wearing a military uniform and appeared to be one of the superior officers.

"Where are you going, boy?"

"I'm looking for Mahmoud."

"Your brother?"

"Yes, my brother."

"Is he a soldier?"

"No, he's a porter at the Alexandria railway station, and he ran in this direction yesterday at the time of the bombardment, shouting, 'Orabi is a real man!'"

"How old is he, and what does he look like?"

"He's fifteen, one year older than I am, but he's thinner and shorter than I am. He was wearing a blue *jilbaab* and a white skullcap. Have you seen him?"

"Go home, my son—go back to your parents, may God compensate them and compensate us."

"Have you seen him?"

When the officer didn't answer, Saïd ran toward the city. "Maybe he's at the station, carrying the passengers' baggage . . . or maybe he went back to his mother . . . or maybe he's standing under the window of the girl he loves . . . I must find him!"

He was running feverishly, while the bombardment convulsed the city, filling up its spaces. He ran until he found himself in the midst of a throng of people hurrying along and creating an uproar. The street was jammed with men, women, and children. The men were cursing the English and calling upon God to bring them to ruin. The women were wailing, the children were crying, and everyone was carrying something, whether small children or possessions or mats or a basket or a cage with a few chickens in it.

Saïd walked with them to he knew not where, since it had become impossible to walk in any other direction, and when the journey seemed to go on and on, he asked an old man who was leading a sheep, "Where are we now, Uncle?"

"We are near the Mahmoudiyya Canal, my son."

"Are we very far from the station?"

"Which station?"

"The railway station."

"We are outside Alexandria, my son. The English have destroyed the forts, and targeted the station and nearby houses. Many have died, and the English just keep on striking, so as to demolish the city entirely. May God destroy their houses, God take revenge on them, God . . ."

"And Orabi, Uncle?"

"Orabi?"

Saïd didn't repeat the question. He plowed through the teeming crowd with difficulty and took a side path, having resolved to return to Alexandria. "I must look for Mahmoud . . . I must find him."

He kept walking among the fields until his head spun, his eyes rolled, and he crumpled up by the side of the road and slept.

In the morning he continued his journey along the route he had chosen, which seemed to him very long. Each time he felt sure he was close to Alexandria, he found himself once again surrounded by fields.

The sun was about to set when he encountered a man leading a water buffalo and a mule. Before Saïd could ask him for directions, the man hailed him with a greeting and asked, "Where are you going, boy?"

"To Alexandria."

"And why to Alexandria, boy, when the English are attacking it? Are you planning to defend it?"

"I'm looking for my friend. I have to get back to Alexandria to find Mahmoud."

"Come, boy—share a bite with me and let me hear your story."

Saïd stretched out on the ground with the man, who placed before them a loaf of bread, a piece of cheese, and two onions. They sat and ate, and Saïd told him what had happened.

"Do you think Mahmoud may have met with some terrible accident, 'Amm Abu Ibrahim?"

"Chin up, be a man, and hear me well. I've left my children in the village to join Orabi's army. I'll send you to them. Tell them you met up with me and that I want you to live with them until I return from the war."

The man stood up and went to get a mat from the back of the mule. He spread it out.

"Now we'll sleep, and in the morning I'll tell you the way to the village."

When Saïd knocked on the door, Umm Ibrahim opened it. She was clearly agitated as she said in a faint voice, "In the name of God the merciful and compassionate—who are you, boy?"

"I am Saïd, and I've just come from Abu Ibrahim . . . I met him when he was on the way to join Orabi's army."

"Welcome! Come in."

No sooner had Saïd entered than the children, as well as a diminutive old woman, gathered around him, eager to hear what he had to say. The children began to pepper him with questions about Alexandria and Orabi and the English ships. Placing food before Saïd, Umm Ibrahim said to her children, "Let him eat and rest—all in good time." And although Saïd had not eaten anything all day, nor even touched the provisions Abu Ibrahim had given to him tied up in a handkerchief, he was not hungry. Rather, he felt a heaviness in his head, a searing pain in his eyes, and a feebleness in his joints.

He put his head down on the mat and fell into a deep sleep. Observing him, Umm Ibrahim said, "Poor thing, he's overcome with fatigue." But during the night she found that Saïd was delirious. She put her hand on his forehead: he was burning with fever.

For the five days that Saïd spent feverish and ill, Umm Ibrahim tended him, as fearful and anxious as if he had been one of her own children. She didn't know whether the reason for her powerful feelings toward him was that he was "a stranger, some mother's son," or whether it was the resemblance—which had struck her the moment she opened the door to him—between him and Ibrahim, who had died: the same age, height, and dark complexion. The children noticed it as well, and pointed it out to the wife of their grandfather, who said, "It could be a devil—be careful of him!" They laughed.

Like Umm Ibrahim, the children loved Saïd and worried over his safe recovery. Even the little girl, Lauza, ten months old, crawled to the mat where Saïd lay, and was content to sit nowhere but by his side.

Sitt Sajar was the only member of the family who didn't welcome him, and she persisted in her doubts about his character. "Only devils have no origins, no known father or mother or country . . . and this island he says he came from—no one's heard of it. I've heard of Cairo, and the Hejaz, and Suez, and the Sudan, but I haven't heard of anything else!"

"And Alexandria, Sitti Sajar?"

"Alexandria!"

The old woman said skeptically, "I've never heard of it—even the name is strange!"

With a naughty wink to his siblings, one of the children said, "Maybe it's the land of the devils, Sitti!"

"God only knows!"

The children laughed, and Sitt Sajar exclaimed angrily, "Ignorant brats!"

On the day of Saïd's recovery, when the fever had left his body, Umm Ibrahim killed a chicken for him and ordered the children to leave it all for him. "The boy is weak," she said, "and his body is depleted. God willing, when your father returns in safety, I'll kill three chickens for you." The children followed their mother when she went to kill the chicken, pluck it, wash it, and boil it. They watched Saïd drinking the broth and eating the delicious meat, but not one of them asked for any.

Saïd lived with Umm Ibrahim as if he was one of her children, of whom there were six: four boys, the eldest of whom was six years younger than he, and two girls, one who still lisped when she talked and the other not yet walking. Each morning the boys went to Qur'an school, and from there they went in the afternoon to work in the field. They were greatly astonished to learn that Saïd had never picked up a hoe in his life, and their amazement grew when he told them that in his country it was slaves who tilled the soil.

"And what does your father do?"

"My father died a few months after I was born."

"But what did he use to do before he died?"

"He was a diver."

"What does that mean, 'a diver'?"

"He would dive into the sea and gather oysters."

"What are oysters?"

"They're shells that are closed up tight, and when you open them you find inside them smooth, gleaming white balls. These balls are pearls, and some of them are very valuable, worth more than gold."

"So was your father rich, then?"

"The pearls didn't belong to my father."

"Why not? Didn't he hunt for them himself?"

"He used to dive with other divers to the bottom of the sea. Each diver carried a knife. One end of a rope was tied to his waist, and someone who stayed on board the boat held onto the other end. The diver would jump into the water and dive, while the person holding the rope would let out the line. When the dive was done, he would pull the line up. The diver would come back up to the ship, his collecting pouch full of oysters, which the ship's captain would take and set aside to give to the Sultan, who would pay the captain and the divers their day's wages."

"And he wouldn't give them any pearls?"

"No."

"Not even one pearl?"

"No."

"How strange!

"And how does a diver breathe when he's underwater?"

"He holds his breath the whole time he's underwater."

"What if he can't?"

"He suffocates and drowns, which is what happened to my father."

"That's a very hard job—farming is easier!"

But Saïd didn't find farming easier. It was easier to go into the sea, hold your breath for several minutes, and then get out and go back on board ship, than it was to strike the earth with your hoe day after day, plough it, sow it with seed, water it, and watch over it for months, then return to work for weeks on end harvesting its crop.

But for all that, Saïd learned to wield a hoe and work with the boys in the field after their return from school. While they were gone, he would go over the alphabet, which they had taught him, or bring fresh water from the pump that was at the other end of the village, or go to the market to sell the eggs that Umm Ibrahim's chickens had laid, or play with the two little girls. He got on close terms with the villagers and the household, all but Sitt Sajar, who grumbled constantly because Abu Ibrahim had taken the water buffalo and deprived them of its milk, and the mule as well, so that she was forced to go to the field on foot. She kept repeating, "Umm Ibrahim, wretched woman, your husband has deceived you . . . says he'll take the water buffalo and the mule to Orabi—he's gone to take a second wife on you in another town!"

Saïd's days passed in peace, harmony, and contentment, always concluding with the evening session of conviviality and laughter with the children. They told him about the blind sheikh who instructed them at school, and the stories and anecdotes that went around. For his part, he told them about the sea and the great ships that carved their paths through waves high as mountains, and about the whale that threatened the whaler, or the one that the sea cast up dead near the beaches, and that they would pull out in order to open its belly and extract the ambergris from it. The party would wind up each night with Saïd telling one of Ammar's tales, expressly chosen by the children.

"The tale of the lion and the fox." "The tale of the frog with two wives." "The tale of the man who felt sorry for a snake being pursued by a farmer, so he gave it refuge in his belly." The children knew all of Ammar's stories; likewise, they knew Ammar himself, as well as Amina and Hafez, as if they had lived with them just like Saïd.

They would carry on talking and laughing until sleep got the better of them. But in his sleep Saïd would not chatter or laugh. He would see Mahmoud running, getting farther and farther away, and he would call out to him, call out and cry. Sometimes he would wake up with traces of tears in his eyes. He wished he would see Mahmoud in his dream, coming toward him: his brown skin and shining eyes, his laughing features and slender build, his blue *jilbaab*, his voice, his walk, and his manner, clear and whole. Saïd told himself, "If this dream comes to me, then Mahmoud is alive and well." The days passed, and Saïd waited for this vision to appear to him in his sleep.

ഇ ഇ ഇ

The cry rose up suddenly in the empty air, and then subsided into silence. It wasn't a cry for help or one of terror, but rather the release of an anguished, weary voice, or something else unfamiliar to Saïd. He listened attentively, but now there was nothing so present, audible, and palpable as the silence that dignified and affirmed the cry he had heard. He went outside to investigate.

He walked, staring at doorways, looking for the afflicted house. The alleyway appeared deserted and silent, but the sound was coming to him now as a muffled drone like the rasp of someone choking or the guttural moans of a woman in the agonies of labor. He walked toward the sound, but then thought it was behind him, so he turned around and went back the other way, only to find that it was coming

23

from yet another direction. Was it one of those innumerable devils that occupied the imagination of Sitt Sajar, or had some inexplicable sorrow settled like a contagion upon the houses?

Among the men he would surely find the answer. He walked in the direction of the fields. The air felt tight and the sun pressed its fire down upon the dust of the road. He felt its sting on his bare feet. He raised the hem of his *jilbaab*, dried the sweat from his face, and kept walking.

It was midday. He looked at the sky as if to ascertain that the sun had reached its zenith. He would find the men gathered beneath the eastern willow, having their lunch, and he would ask them. But what if the cry had been a figment of his imagination? And what of the droning sound? No, he wouldn't ask them. He would sit among them enjoying their company, and when they got up to work, he would take up a hoe and labor with them, cultivating the earth. Umm Ibrahim would scold him for having left the two little girls alone in the house with no one to look after them. He stopped once again, lifted the hem of his *jilbaab*, and wiped his face.

He didn't find anyone at the eastern willow or anywhere near it. He searched the fields with his eyes, but saw only an untethered donkey and a water buffalo yoked to a stationary waterwheel. The ploughed fields were entirely abandoned, apart from the egrets that would alight here and there on the furrows that had been dug.

He ran back to the village. The closer he got to it, the clearer the sounds were. This was no droning, but rather a wail that rose and intensified. Then he saw the women who had climbed to the roofs of the houses and were tearing their cheeks, beating their breasts, and rending their clothing; or else they were seizing the edges of their veils in their fists and yanking them this way and that, in a rhythmic twitch that matched the cadence of their cries of lamentation. From time to time they would be interrupted by a sudden shrill wail from one or another of the women, who would leap spastically about, like a newly killed chicken.

Saïd walked from one alleyway to the next, his eyes fixed upon the roofs of the houses, and their façades like speaking human faces enveloped by the blackness and the cacophony of mourning. He stopped to wipe away the salty moisture that flowed from his pores and covered his face and eyes. The women's sorrow convulsed his guts, but he kept walking until he had traversed all the alleyways of the village. Then he stopped, perplexed. He pushed open the door to one of the houses and came upon some men and boys he didn't know. He sat down with them, and, like them, was silent.

      ဢ   ဢ   ဢ

Orabi had lost the war. And what if Abu Ibrahim had gone the way of Mahmoud? The question kept him awake night after night. Despite the warmth of September, his body was rigid with cold, which prevented him from sleeping through the night.

But 'Amm Abu Ibrahim did not stay away like Mahmoud. He pushed open the door with his staff one evening, and came in, to the jubilant shouts of the children. Umm Ibrahim, smiling radiantly, said, "If I wouldn't be scolded for it, I would trill for joy!"[7]

Sitt Sajar said, "Where are the mule and the water buffalo, Abu Ibrahim?"

One of the children spoke up, reminding his mother, "When will you kill the three chickens?"

Abu Ibrahim didn't answer his father's wife. He rebuked his son, then looked kindly at Saïd and asked him how he was. Then he asked his wife to heat water for his bath. He bathed, then lay down on his mat and slept.

Umm Ibrahim confided her worries to Saïd as they were returning from the Thursday market. "You didn't know Abu Ibrahim before he went away. He was cheerful and patient, an easygoing and generous man, the best. He laughed with the children and spent companionable evenings with them. But now, as you see, he doesn't open his mouth except to scold them or threaten them with beatings, or else he keeps silent as if he'd forgotten how to talk. Sitt Sajar says to him, 'Orabi put a hex on you.' You all laugh, but sometimes I tell myself maybe she's right, or else he's ill."

"He could be ill, Umm Ibrahim . . . wasn't I sick for five days after I arrived from Alexandria?"

"You were sick, and you recovered, because you did as I told you to do. As for him, he doesn't listen, and he eats less than my daughter Lauza—how can he get his health back if he doesn't eat?"

Saïd tried to reassure her. He told her that Orabi had lost the war, and that Abu Ibrahim was grieving because of that, and grieving also because, surely, he had comrades who had died in the war. "But even grief gets lighter in time." And Saïd told her for the first time about Mahmoud—how he had gone off and how Saïd had looked for him but not found him. Umm Ibrahim began to cry, wiping her tears away with her sleeve.

Saïd knew that everything Umm Ibrahim had said was true, for every day he saw how irritable Abu Ibrahim was with his children, how he scolded and beat them. It was true that he was kind to Saïd, treating him differently from the others, but otherwise his presence in the house wrapped its occupants in a gloom Saïd had not known there in Abu Ibrahim's absence. Even the nightly amusements—the conversation and the laughter—came to an end, because they were afraid of him.

Once during the long months Saïd heard Abu Ibrahim laughing: laughing loudly and from his heart. He had been out of the house, and the children were singing. They stopped when he walked in on them. He asked one of them, "What were you singing, boy?"

"I wasn't singing."

"Oh, yes you were singing—I heard you. What were you singing?"

The child hesitated, then confessed:

> Hey, Seymour, you lousy-face,
> Who told you you could have this place?[8]

Smiling, his father asked him, "Do you know who Seymour is?"

"An Englishman, of course!"

Abu Ibrahim laughed, and the children laughed to see him laugh. Umm Ibrahim left her trough of dough to join them, traces of the dough still on her hands, and laughed along with them.

The children asked, "So, should we sing, Papa?"

"Sing."

So the children sang, turning around and around in the courtyard of the house:

> Hey, Seymour, you lousy-face,
> Who told you you could have this place?

Their voices rose higher than before, their enthusiasm roused because their father was laughing, laughing for the first time in months. Umm Ibrahim returned to her baking trough, saying, "Oh, God, make him well again."

ം   ം   ം

Saïd stayed for a year in Abu Ibrahim's house, as if he was one of his children. During the final month, however, he missed his mother intensely, as she began coming to him in his dreams. And he longed for the sea, which he conjured up in his imagination. Meanwhile, he also missed Hafez more and more, as well as Ammar, and the island and its people, who were constantly in his thoughts. When he could endure his longing no more, he bade farewell to Abu Ibrahim and his family, and set out for Suez, to look for a ship heading southward.

Umm Ibrahim wept when the time came for his departure. "It's as if you were a child of my womb, Saïd," she said. The two little girls clung to him, wanting to go with him. Abu Ibrahim and the boys accompanied him to where the Suez road began. He told them good-bye, holding the basket that Umm Ibrahim had filled with bread she had baked especially for him, and set off on his journey.

CHAPTER FOUR

Ammar's Reminiscences

ഗ്ര

In recent months Ammar had been much given to thinking about the past—about his mother and father, and his brothers and sisters, whose names, or even how many they had been, he no longer recalled. He remembered indistinct sounds like speech, or humming, or songs chanted by a woman as she turned a hand mill or pounded a wooden mortar, and a space in which the colors orange and green mingled—was it the leaves of the banana plants, incandescent in the midday glare, or his mother's dress, or the mango fruits with their rinds scattered about him as he devoured them? Ammar stared intently, but saw only a light, in the midst of which the faces were clouded. Yet they pressed upon him all the same, for the moment of death was drawing near, and the hour of reunion was at hand; but would he be lost to them in the hereafter as he had been lost here on earth, and find himself alone in the land of the dead, not knowing his own kin?

Ammar was in his seventies, or perhaps his eighties—he wasn't sure, but he did know that in the beginning he had been with them, and then the ship had taken him away with some others, and he had become one of the slaves belonging to the Sultan of Zanzibar. He remembered his adolescence on the clove plantations, and the words of the Sultan of Zanzibar as he presented him to Sultan Khalid: "This is my slave, Ammar, whom God has graced with a comely face, a sturdy physique, and a tall frame, and cleverness as well—such wonders there are in God's creation!—for he is swift like an arrow, and as accurate. Add him to your quiver, for he is my gift to you."

And so on returning to this island, Sultan Khalid had brought him with him in his ship. And Ammar had not wept as on his first journey; on the contrary, he took pride in the words spoken by the Sultan of Zanzibar and in Sultan Khalid's decision to make him his personal servant.

How much time had passed? Khalid had died and been succeeded by his elder son, Aliaddin, but his brother, Nu'maan, had murdered him and taken control of the island. Ammar grew old, and no one delegated to him any longer the many important tasks that had been assigned to him before. He became a retired slave, leaning on his cane just to walk a few steps, or sitting near the kitchen courtyard hoping for someone to come and exchange a word with him. He wished he could go to the fields, where there were many slaves, so that he could get together with them and pass the time in their company, playing with their little ones and chatting with the old men among them. But his legs were no longer capable of carrying him well enough for him to descend the hill and cross the island, then retrace his steps and climb the hill once more.

They had envied him because he was the Sultan's personal servant, which exempted him from backbreaking labor in the fields, sunup to sundown, and kept him out of the way of the whips wielded by the princes who supervised the plantations and managed their production. He had likewise considered himself fortunate, but he wondered now whether they hadn't been better off: they lived together, sharing their lives, marrying and having children and filling the land around them with their seed, while he remained like a solitary tree in a desolate land that would find none to come after him once he was felled by death. If he had had a son or a daughter, a wife and grandchildren, he would have awaited their arrival after his death, knowing that no matter how long he must wait, they would come, and he would not be alone in death as he had been in life.

"I must remember my mother's face . . . I must." Ammar repeated this to himself as he stared into the past, but nothing came to him except indistinct voices in a space where the colors green and orange mingled.

Amina saw him as she was moving the sacks of flour, and she puzzled over his presence there at that time of day. He was leaning his head against a stone, his eyes closed. She called to him, "Ammar!"

He opened his eyes. "Amina?"

"Good morning! What brings you here so early in the day?"

"It was very hot last night, and I couldn't sleep. Has Saïd returned?"

"He hasn't returned, although many ships come into port these days, and I go there every day to inquire."

"Saïd will come back to you, Amina; God willing, he'll come back. I saw it in a dream." Ammar hadn't seen any such thing, but he wanted to reassure her.

Amina left the sacks of flour and sat down beside him. "What did you see, and when, and why didn't you tell me?"

"Just now, sitting here, I dozed off, and I saw Saïd, none other than he—would I mistake him? He was climbing the hill and calling for you."

"Calling for me in distress?"

"He was climbing the hill, returning from his travels and bringing you a gift from a distant land. He was smiling, and he had grown a mustache like a man's."

"He had grown a man's mustache? You saw that, Ammar?"

"I swear I did, Amina!"

Ammar found nothing wrong in swearing this oath, for he felt he was telling the truth, even though he had not seen Saïd in a dream. He wanted to prolong their conversation, so he asked her, "You said that many ships have been coming to the port—what ships?"

"English ships. They are setting up a base on the eastern side of the island, and they've begun construction on it."

"A base?"

"A base for their army."

"And why are the English posting an army among us, Amina?"

"I don't know, Ammar."

She said good-bye to him and got up to move the sacks of flour and commence her day's work. He stayed where he was, sorry that she had gone.

Amina resembled her mother. If he let his mind wander in time, he could have sworn that the woman who had been seated beside him had been Maliha, and not her daughter. Beautiful Maliha, with her two braids, her dimple, her radiant face. He used to follow her, and she would say, "Go away, Ammar!"

"How can I go away?"

"Go away!" she would say, laughing.

But he didn't go away, even after she became a wife and mother, even after she died. For how could he go away, and where should he go?

"Would you agree to marry me, Maliha?" he had asked her once.

"And who better than you on this island, Ammar?"

He went to the Sultan and asked to be released to marry her. "Release me," he said, "and I will remain your slave for life." Had his father, Sultan Khalid, been alive, he would have agreed, for he was not so cruel. This sultan he had carried on his back when he was a child and run with him from the fortress to the port, from the port to the fortress, while the boy wrapped his legs around Ammar's neck, prodding him with them as if on horseback, and laughing, his peals of laughter resounding all over the hillside. He had carried him on his back, and told him stories, bathed him with his own hands and poured rosewater on his body before he went to lie with his first woman. An ungrateful dog he was—sleeping with countless women, master of the island and all who lived upon it—who begrudged Ammar one woman. Maliha, who had taken possession of his heart, and Nu'maan bereaved him of her by refusing to release him.

When Amina's husband, Abdullah, died, leaving her a lone girl and Saïd in her arms still nursing, he was tempted by the idea of marrying her. He asked his friend Jaafar, the judge's slave, to ask his master whether it was permissible for a man to marry his wife's daughter, whereupon Jaafar pointed out that he had not married Maliha, and that Amina was therefore not his wife's daughter. "You could marry Amina, Ammar. But would the Sultan release you?" He had no intention of asking the Sultan to release him. If Amina accepted him, he would take her and Saïd on a fishing boat and with them flee the island and its ungrateful sultan, who had forgotten how Ammar used to carry him on his shoulders and run with him like a horse. But he didn't flee, nor did he propose marriage to Amina. He saw Maliha in a dream, a frown of displeasure on her face, so he knew that it would be against her wishes, and that it was not permissible for a man to marry his wife's daughter.

He saw Amina leaving the kitchen courtyard, on her way home. "Amina . . ."

"Are you still sitting there, Ammar?"

"I was enjoying the breeze, so I stayed."

"And you haven't eaten anything since morning?"

"I'm not hungry."

She sat down beside him, opened her kerchief, and gave him one of the two loaves it contained. "You must eat. You'll get even weaker without food."

"When Saïd comes back, Amina, find him a wife."

"Find him a wife?"

"Do you want him to end up like me, cut off with no wife or children?"

"But Saïd is still young, Ammar."

"He's not so young. I saw him in my dream, and his mustache had grown."

"Tell me about the dream, Ammar."

"I told you what I saw."

"Tell me more."

"He was bringing you a gift."

"Did you see it?"

"I couldn't make it out. He was covering it with his hand. Are you going to visit Maliha's grave, Amina?"

"I went last year."

"Go to visit her, Amina."

"I'll go, Ammar."

She helped him to his feet and accompanied him part of his way, then turned to go down the hill. Ammar carried on in the direction of his room in the cellars of the fortress, where he lived with the Sultan's servants. He was thinking, as he walked slowly, leaning on his cane, that the dead need us as much as we need them. If we were never to go and ask after them, they would be oppressed by sorrow and crushed by loneliness. He could not visit the graves of his mother and father, since he didn't know in what land they had been buried. He wondered, did his brothers and sisters go to them and ask after them, and alleviate something of their loneliness, or had other ships carried them off to become slaves in foreign parts, cut off like the branches of a tree?

CHAPTER FIVE

The Ringdove

ဢၣ

S he heard someone whispering her name, and when she peered into the darkness in the direction of the sound, she recognized her paternal cousin Hafez. She was puzzled that he should call to her in a whisper, and not approach her where she sat weaving palm leaves by the light of the moon. She stood up to go to him.

"What's come over you, Hafez? You stand there frozen like a statue, hissing like a viper, 'Ta–wad-dud . . .'"

She mimicked him teasingly, but he didn't laugh. "Tawaddud, can you keep a secret?"

"What secret?"

"Swear you'll keep it, and I'll tell you."

"I'll keep it."

Hafez reached into his pocket and drew out a folded paper. "I want you to deliver this letter to someone at the plantations, and to keep it confidential and not tell anyone about the matter."

"Who wrote the letter?" Hafez could not read or write.

"Someone you don't know."

"What's in it?"

"I don't know!"

She laughed in disbelief.

"Tawaddud, this is an important letter, and there's none among the women of this quarter more suitable than you to convey it."

She was pleased by the flattery. "Are you joking?"

"I'm not joking."

"Then tell me what's written in the letter, and I'll take it."

"I don't know."

"So why don't you take it yourself?"

"Because it would look suspicious for me to go to one of the women slaves at the plantations."

"Which woman?"

"The one you're taking the letter to."

"The letter is written to a woman?"

She raised her voice in asking this question, and it seemed to Hafez that she was protesting, that she didn't believe him.

"And does this woman know how to read?"

"I don't know."

Impatient, Tawaddud mimicked him. "'I don't know!' I won't take the letter. Find yourself a mule to take it!" She left him, went back to her place, and sat down to weave the palm leaves, absorbed in her task as if he was not standing a few meters away waiting to continue the discussion.

She heard his footsteps as he came toward her, but she didn't raise her eyes from her work. He sat down beside her, silent.

"What's the woman's name?"

He told her.

"Is your friend in love with her?"

He said nothing.

"Have you forgotten how to talk?"

"If I tell you I don't know, you'll get angry. My friend didn't tell me he was in love with her. Maybe he is in love with her. Maybe he doesn't know her. Maybe he heard of her skill in mixing medicinal herbs and he wants a potion for himself or for his mother or father. Or it could be that the letter isn't intended for her, but for her son or her brother or her husband. I don't know!"

"Give me the letter."

He handed her the folded paper and told her the way to go, warning her of the need for caution. Then he laughed, and said, "When I go to India, I'll bring you a white elephant in return for your help!"

Tawaddud laughed as she saw him off. Hafez was repeating the expression she had used with him when he was a small child. He had been four or five years old and she was at least ten when she had told him, "If you behave yourself and do as you're told, I'll bring you a white elephant from India."

"How will you get to India, Tawaddud?" he asked her.

She replied confidently, "I'll go to India, to Sind, and beyond. And you'll see for yourself when I come back from my travels, bringing marvels with me."

She had been in the habit of dreaming about traveling to faraway countries. And why shouldn't she dream, when the door of her hut opened onto the sea with its great waves, while ships came and went and the mariners around her filled the island with the sights they had seen on their journeys, and the stories they had to tell painted the days and nights in colors more brilliant than those of the sunrise.

She dreamed until the day she made up her mind. She hid behind a tree, cut her hair, and put on one of her brother's *jilbaabs*. Then she went to the port, where she met a ship's captain and claimed to be a youth looking for work. The captain said, "You're still young, lad. Come back after two years and I'll give you a job." But before two years had gone by, what she had not counted upon came to pass: her breasts matured and her buttocks grew round, and no longer could any seaman, no matter how dim his eyesight, mistake her for a boy.

Amina didn't understand why men love the sea, and Tawaddud couldn't understand why Amina didn't understand. For what else should a person love, on an island ringed by beaches like a necklace, and the sea beyond them swelling and reaching to the countries of the wide world?

She looked at the folded paper in her hands, then hid it in her bosom and stood up. She tiptoed into the hut and groped her way in the dark between her sleeping family members. She got her box and returned to her place under the moonlight.

She opened the box and took out the book. She ran her hand over its cover, then opened it and gazed intently at the series of letters in their graceful and orderly cursive script. She stared and stared, as if the lines might in the end reveal to her their hidden riches.

Her mother used to go regularly to the judge's house. They would place before her piles of clothing: the judge's clothes, as well as those of his son and his wife and daughters. Her mother would bend over the washtub that was the color of the dust from the road. Tawaddud would sit near her, now chattering, now daydreaming, now complaining of boredom, as she waited for her mother to finish the washing and carry the clothes, rinsed and wrung out, to be hung up for drying on the line that was strung in the rear courtyard of the house.

One day when Tawaddud saw the judge's wife and daughters leaving the house, an idea flashed through her mind. She slipped from her place and went to have a look. She made her way unsteadily to a spacious hall, its floor covered with soft, silken carpets whose texture she could feel with her bare feet, beautiful carpets whose splendid colors wound and twisted sinuously in strange patterns. She looked at the carpets, and then she looked at the ceiling. Unlike the ceilings of the huts, which rose only two or three hand-spans above the head, this ceiling was so lofty it could not be reached by a giant standing on another giant's shoulders! Even the chandeliers strung on iron chains that hung from the ceiling were likewise so high as to be out of hands' reach. Tawaddud stared at the carpets, then at the ceiling, and then she circled the room with her eyes, discovering the couches covered with cushions and rugs, and the wooden wardrobes inlaid with shell.

Then she heard a melodious voice. It wasn't reciting the Qur'an, but it was reciting something. She walked in the direction of the voice, and saw through an open door the judge sitting cross-legged on a couch with a book in his hands from which he was reading to his son. To one side, she saw the walls of the room covered with shelves bearing a great many books bound with leather covers, black, green, blue, and red, their spines inscribed with gold lettering that fascinated her. The reading held her in thrall, such that she forgot about her mother and about the one-eyed judge's face, which had always frightened her.

She stood and listened until she heard her mother calling for her, and then she hurried toward her before the judge should become aware of her presence.

She spent the whole day thinking, until her mind hit upon a plan. She proceeded to go over it again and again, throughout the night, until she heard the rooster crow, at which point she left, sneaking out of the hut. She stood behind a tree near the judge's house until she saw him go out to attend the dawn prayer. Then she stole up to the house and went into the room where he had been sitting the previous day. It was dark in there, and it was impossible for her to see or sense the books. She hid underneath the couch and began to wait.

Sleep overcame her, and she was oblivious until roused by the sound of a maid who had come to clean. She suppressed the sound of her breathing, and kept waiting. Then came the call to midday prayer. Time passed, and then she heard the judge's footsteps approaching, and she sensed the weight of his body as he sat down on the couch. Despite the murky shadows, the cold marble, and the awkwardness of her prone position, the only thing that bothered her was the audible pounding of her heart, and her fear that the sound would reach the judge's ears, where he sat directly above her.

The judge read to his son about the dove known as the ringdove,[1] the leader of the doves, and how she and her small companions were caught in a hunter's net. The judge read: "Each of the doves began to struggle in her own part of the net, trying to effect her own escape.

The ringdove said, 'Do not abandon one another in your struggle! Let not the soul of any one of you assume a greater importance than that of her companion. Rather, let us cooperate, and then perhaps we can unfasten the net and rescue one another.' They did so, by their cooperation unfastening the net, and they flew with it high into the sky."

"Daddy, I need to pee."

Was this any time to pee?! The judge stopped reading and the boy went out.

A silly, oafish child, interrupting the melodious reading and the thread of the lovely story with his annoying whine. Tawaddud's heart was consumed with rage, although she stayed motionless in her place under the couch. This stupid boy—how could he feel an urge to go to the bathroom while the fate of the ringdove hung in the balance?

At last the boy came back, and the judge continued. The ringdove flew, she and her companions bearing the net, until they reached the ringdove's friend, the rat. The judge read on:

"The ringdove called out his name—which was Zairek—and he answered her from his burrow, saying, 'Who are you?'

"She replied, 'Your good friend the ringdove.'

"He hurried out to meet her, and when he saw her in the net, he said to her, 'My sister, how did you come to be in this predicament, and you among the shrewdest of creatures?'

"She said to him, 'Don't you know that nothing of good or evil befalls any of us other than that which is enjoined upon us by fate? In the full course of our days, whatever our weaknesses or our strengths, each of us will be tested, whether in poverty or prosperity. So it is destiny that put me in this predicament, that drew me to the bait, and hid the net from me so that I got caught in it, together with my companions.'"

The judge continued, "Then the rat began to gnaw on the knot that bound the ringdove. She said to him, 'Start with the knot that is holding the doves in front of me, before attending to me.' She repeated this to him again and again, but for all that, he paid no heed to what she said.

"When she pressed him, he said to her, 'You have been saying the same thing over and over, as if your own soul were not in need, or as if you accorded it no rights.'

"The ringdove replied, 'Do not blame me for what I ask of you: for I was entrusted with the leadership of the rest, and that is an awesome responsibility. And I may earn their respect and compliance by first deferring to and assisting them: thus may God deliver us from the hunter. Moreover, I fear that if you were to start by gnawing the knot that binds me, you would grow weary and bored, and some of those who are with me would be left behind. But I know that if you should begin with them, leaving me till last, you would not be satisfied—even if you were overcome by torpor and fatigue—until you had set me free of my bonds.'

"The rat said to her, 'This is yet another quality that adds to the esteem and affection that your admirers feel for you.' With that he resumed gnawing on the net until he had finished, so that the ringdove and the other doves escaped and went back to where they had come from."

"Daddy, I'm hungry."

"Can't you wait until I read to you how the raven got to know the rat, and what transpired between them?"

"My stomach is aching with hunger."

"We'll continue on the day after tomorrow, then."

Tawaddud waited until the judge and his son had left. Then she hurried out of the house. No sooner had she gotten well away from it than she began to leap about, dancing with delight and singing for joy. When she ran into Saïd and Hafez, she said she would make a small palm leaf basket for each of them. The boys sat down beside her, breathless, as she swiftly and skillfully wove the palm leaves together.

Two days later Tawaddud went back again and hid under the couch. The wait seemed shorter than it had on the previous occasion, for she passed the time by going over in her head the part of the story that she had heard. What, pray, would happen next? What was this friendship that was to develop between the raven and the rat, and what would the two of them do?

She wished the story would go on and on, indeed, that it would never end, even if she spent the rest of her days lying there cramped under the couch.

The judge came and recounted to his son how the rat and the raven met and went together to see the tortoise. Tawaddud, who had been drawn by the thread of the tale from the beginning, was now captivated by the speech of the animals, who spoke with wisdom and wove their discourse with an astonishing skill that surpassed her own skill in weaving palm leaves.

The rat told his troubles to the tortoise, who advised him to forget his loneliness and desolation. She said, "Use your knowledge, and don't bemoan your penury. For a man of valor may be blessed with other things besides wealth—like the lion, who is feared even when lying down; while the rich man who possesses no courage is despised even as his wealth increases—like the dog, who is despised even if bedecked with bracelets and anklets. And don't exaggerate your loneliness, for the wise man feels nowhere alienated or alone, nor does he stray from home unaccompanied by all he needs of wisdom and courage—like the lion, who does not wander unaccompanied by his strength, by which he lives wherever he may roam."

The raven heard the tortoise's words, and addressed her in his turn. But Tawaddud was unable to follow what the raven said, for she was struggling to suppress a sneeze that threatened to expose her. She held it back, and sighed with relief. She was preparing to find out what happened when a gazelle who was passing by approached the raven, the rat, and the tortoise, but all at once the sneeze escaped from her, convulsing her body and causing her to bump her head on the underside of the couch where the judge was sitting.

Tawaddud found herself sprawled upon the floor, not daring to move her hand to rub the part of her head that hurt. The couch was lifted from its place, and before her eyes Tawaddud saw the judge's slipper. She raised her eyes slowly from his slipper to his robe, and from his robe to his head, and there her gaze was met by the keen eye of the judge. She picked herself up and stood on her feet, preparing to flee, but the judge's hand had her by the collar.

"Who are you, and what are you doing here?"

She was tongue-tied. The judge slapped her twice, his hand almost encircling her head, but before he could let fall a third blow, she slipped from his grasp and took to her heels.

The following day she went to Ammar and asked him to tell her the tale of the ringdove.

"The tale of the ringdove?"

"It's a story the judge was reading to his son from one of the books he has."

"But, Tawaddud, I know nothing of stories written in books!"

Her tears flowed, and she sobbed until her body shook with the force of her weeping. Ammar cajoled her, gave her a piece of sugar, and tried to tell her a different story, but she continued to cry.

For a while her heart was burning with rage, choked with grief, until an idea came to her. She set about its execution the moment she heard the rooster's crow. She crept to the judge's house and waited until he left for the dawn prayer. Then she went into the hall of books, stole a book, and made off with her loot, running back to the hut.

Now she sat by the door meditating upon its blue leather binding, which was bordered by a framework of gold engraving; in the center of this was a calligraphic script, rising in straight lines, leaning at angles, ascending, descending, gracefully flowing. She didn't know whether this was the book whose pages contained the story of the ringdove, but it was a big, beautiful book, and she was pleased with it.

Tawaddud extracted the folded letter, spread it out upon a page of the open book, and gazed at it. Its cursive script was not regular and flowing like the lines engraved upon the book. She stared at it intently. What, she wondered, was written in the letter that she would carry to the plantations the following day?

It was not out of love or affection for Hafez that she had agreed to convey the letter; an avid curiosity, rather—a craving for knowledge—was her motive. For what was the story of this woman? Was she young or old? Did she know how to read and write, and if so, who taught her, and how? There were no women on the entire island who could read, apart from the daughters of the Sultan. Even the judge's daughters had not learned this skill.

Furthermore, Hafez had said that the letter was important, and that he could not find anyone among the women of the district worthier than Tawaddud to convey it. She was pleased by Hafez's words, and by his trust in her ability to see the letter successfully to its destination. And if something bad should happen as a consequence? That didn't worry her. She would do what she could to extricate herself from any predicament.

Tawaddud folded the letter and tucked it back in her bosom. She wiped the book with the hem of her robe and placed it in the box. Then she carried it to the hut and put it back in its place.

She stretched out on the mat beside her sleeping family, and lay there listening to the roar of the sea. Her imagination carried her, now to a clever rat who gnawed on a formidable net into which a flock of doves had fallen, then to the cautious steps she would take in delivering a letter of whose contents she was ignorant, to a woman whom she did not know.

CHAPTER SIX

The Return of the Wanderer

ℰℭℛ

Saïd took a Dutch ship that stopped in Aden on its way to South Africa. The journey seemed to him long and lonely, for there was no one on board the ship who spoke Arabic, apart from a Greek mariner who knew a few words of it.

When Saïd arrived in Aden, he had to wait several weeks before he could find a boat that would convey him to the island. The wait, though, was not as difficult as the journey had been, for he could talk to people, see the sights of the city and wander in its markets.

Then came an Omani ship returning from the north and destined for Zanzibar and Musqat. Saïd talked to its crew, and they interceded for him with the ship's captain, who agreed that if Saïd worked his passage, they would deliver him to the island. Saïd passed some pleasant moments in the companionship of the Omani sailors, who would sit up each night telling anecdotes and tales of marvels. They talked of the strange sights they had seen in European ports; of conditions in Oman after the state treasuries were depleted and the country was oppressed by its debts; and of what they had heard from African sailors about the atrocities committed by the Europeans in the countries they occupied.

"And you, Saïd, what about you?"

"I was in Alexandria when the English attacked it. I saw their battleships bombarding the forts and destroying them; I saw the people cursing the English and calling on Orabi to defeat them."

"Is Orabi the leader of Egypt?"

"He wasn't the leader of Egypt, but its people love him. He was the commander of their army, and it was he who fought the English, but he was defeated and the English occupied Egypt and sent him into exile."

"An African sailor told me about a conversation that took place between the people of his village and the French missionary who came to the village and settled there. He said, 'The missionary talked to us for hours on end about the beauty and magnificence of his country and the pleasure of life there. We told him, "What you are saying can't be right, for if life in your country is as beautiful as your description, then what brought you all here to plague us this way?" The missionary protested, "But we don't disturb you—we've come to help you, and to teach you." The people of the village said, "Do you help us build our huts?" "No," replied the missionary. They said, "Do you till our soil?" "No," said the missionary. They said, "Do you fashion for us the spears with which we defend ourselves against savage beasts?" "No," said the missionary, "but we build the big ships that you see in the port, and we make guns, which are more deadly than spears." The people of the village said to him, "Fine. Teach us how to build ships and make guns!"'"

The sailors laughed uproariously, and didn't stop until one of them said, "Do you remember Princess Salma, sister of the Sultan of Zanzibar, who ran off with a German officer and married him?"

"That's an old story."

"What's new about it is that she went back to visit Zanzibar under the protection of a German warship. A sailor from Zanzibar told me that she stepped onto the island unveiled like the foreign women, dressed in clothes like theirs, and wearing a hat with a feather in it. She made the rounds of the island, talking to people and visiting whomever she pleased."

"What did her brother do?"

"His hands were tied. He just stood there, watching and containing his rage, for she had come to the island as a high-ranking German citizen. The sailors say she helps the Germans, and that they consult her. As for her brother, the Sultan Barghash, he serves the English and does their bidding. So who knows? Maybe he's afraid the Germans will take over his island and set her up as its sovereign instead of him."

"God almighty."

"Do you remember that pimp who used to procure slave boys for the captains?"

"Wasn't his name also Barghash?"

"That's the one. I saw him at the port in Aden, so I called Hammoud and Khalil and Mohammed, and we gave him such a good thrashing he almost died at our hands."

Hammoud said, "By God, if Khalil and Mohammed hadn't held me back, I'd have left him nothing but a lifeless corpse." Turning to the rest of the group, he clarified, "You don't know his story. This man was a pederast and a pimp—if the filth of his character spread, it would infect the country with rottenness. Ten years ago, we were on a ship like this one, working like God-fearing men, and they gave us rotten food you could see with your own eyes was crawling with maggots. We said, 'We won't eat and we won't work, unless you change the food.' When they didn't comply, we decided to take over the ship. We got everything ready: the rope to tie up the officers, the clubs and knives to defend ourselves with, and we agreed how and when to start. The whole crew was with us, for all of them were oppressed by the idea of working on a ship that bore tons of treasure, while what we were offered even dogs would refuse."

Saïd asked, "And did you take over the ship?"

"Barghash, the dog, he's the one who put a stop to that."

"How?"

"He informed the captain. The captain arrested our leaders, who were condemned to death by firing squad, and he sentenced all the rest of us to fifty lashes."

Saïd replied, "I'm with Hammoud. If I'd been with you and had seen this Barghash, I wouldn't have left him alive, if only in revenge for your comrades who were executed and for the fifty lashes."

An elderly sailor spoke up. "You're young fellows, and the blood runs hot in your veins. When you get older, you'll understand that man doesn't always do what he wishes he'd done, that the evil all around him is stronger than he is and he doesn't have what it takes to overcome it. God alone is the avenger."

Saïd, however, persisted in his stubbornness. "But man doesn't give up his rights, and if what you say is true, then Orabi was wrong to fight the English."

"But he lost, my son."

"But at least he tried, father."

One of the sailors laughed. "We'll call you 'the Egyptian,' Saïd!" he said.

Saïd laughed, pleased by the appellation.

ဢ   ဢ   ဢ

Saïd's eyes fixed upon a point on the horizon that grew until the familiar palms appeared, as well as the rocky hillside, and the beaches twisted and curved in their ancient congress with the sea. The land drew nearer as Saïd watched, and the seagulls scattered their whiteness in the blue of sky and sea.

Then the ship moored, and Saïd disembarked. In his hand was the basket that Umm Ibrahim had filled with bread for him, into which he had placed two *jilbaabs*, a pair of slippers, two *rotls* of coffee beans purchased in Yemen, and the gift he had brought for his mother from Egypt.

He met a young girl playing near the house. He asked her, "Is Amina at home?"

"Who are you, and why do you ask?"

"I'm Saïd . . ."

She stared at him, then smiled. "I didn't recognize you. Don't you know me?"

Then she told him her name and the names of her mother and father. He laughed. "Of course I didn't recognize you! When I left, you were two feet tall. Now you've grown to twice that height!"

The girl laughed, saying as she ran off, "I'll go tell your mother!"

Amina stared at the girl in amazement, as if she was speaking an unknown language. A few seconds passed before she took off like an arrow. How did she cover the distance? Whom did she see on her way? Did anyone speak to her or ask her why she was running? Did she reply, and if so, what did she say? Did the girl run with her or did she stay behind in the kitchen? Amina had no answers to these questions; she knew none. And anyone who caught sight of her along the way saw nothing of her but two legs running and two braids flying in the wind, as she raised up her voice calling to Saïd and the echo resounded over the hillside.

Saïd heard her voice and ran in its direction. Then he saw her and ran harder. She threw her arms around him and wept. She kissed his head, his brow, and his shoulders. Then she stepped back two paces and surveyed him, before clasping him to her breast once more. She took him by the hand and drew him into the hut, seating him beside her. "You've grown taller, Saïd," she said, "your shoulders have broadened, and you've a man's mustache." She laughed, and so did he.

Amina prepared his old slippers and his *jilbaab*—according to her habit, she had washed it, folded it, and placed it under his bed. The robe didn't extend past his knees, and the slippers were only half the size of his feet. She was laughing and crying, standing up and then sitting down, touching him and gazing at him, asking him questions, her face lightening and darkening, her cheeks by turns rosy, then pale, then rosy again.

She went in haste to her neighbor to borrow some flour, then lit a fire and began to bake a flat-cake for Saïd. He gazed at her, then said, "You've grown more beautiful, Amina."

She looked at him, her face breaking into a radiant smile, which brought out the dimples in her cheeks. "It nearly killed me, having you so far away, Saïd," she said.

She asked him about his journey going and coming, where he had lived and how, whether he had kept the amulet she had made for him . . .

She sat there, close to him, following his narrative until she heard the neighbor's rooster crow, at which point she insisted that he get some sleep. He lay down on his bed and she tucked the covers around him. She sat beside him, gazing at his face as it succumbed to sleep, then she got up to go to work.

On the threshold between waking and sleeping, Saïd followed her with his eyes, contemplating the loveliness of her face, her tall and slender frame, and her black hair, braided like horses' tails. He found her glowing, radiant, her face illuminated by the orange shawl he had bought for her in Egypt, as well as by her joy at their reunion.

Amina had gone a few steps before she remembered Ammar. "He's the one who told me, Saïd—it was he who saw your return in a dream. I'll let him know that you've come back, and I'll tell him that you'll go to visit him." Then she left, the orange shawl covering her head and falling to the middle of her back.

Saïd didn't sleep. Instead he went for a walk on the island. He headed first to the fishermen's beach to ask after Hafez, who, they told him, had gone out fishing. He met a number of the older fishermen, whom he recognized, and he was surprised that they did not recognize him in turn. He kept repeating, "I'm Saïd, Saïd son of Amina the baker!" They laughed in surprise and said, "You've grown up, Saïd. You've come to look like your grandfather—how could we not have recognized you?"

Saïd left them and walked southward until he came to the palm groves. He passed them by and proceeded to the fields, but he didn't get too close, for he knew that it was forbidden for anyone to enter them, except for the plantation slaves, the princes, and their assistants who supervised the plantations.

He walked on, taking a route adjacent to the farms. He passed fields of cotton and corn, fields of clove, banana groves, and orchards of carob and tamarind. From a distance he saw the slaves bending over the earth, just as he had done with 'Amm Abu Ibrahim and his children. Then he retraced his steps to the palm groves, stretched out in the shade of a palm tree, and slept.

He woke after the sun had begun to set, and hastened back to the house, where he found his mother waiting for him. "I asked myself," she said, "was it a dream, Amina? Have you taken leave of your senses? Has your heart conjured up Saïd's homecoming for you? Come and eat, Saïd. I've baked you a flat-cake the likes of which I've never in my life made before. When Umm Latif learned that you'd come back, she gave me some sugar and raisins to make it for you."

They sat and ate. Amina was laughing as she described to him how the women couldn't take their eyes off the shawl. "Tawaddud said to me, 'If Saïd brought me a shawl like that, I'd marry him instantly!'"

"Does she still refuse to get married?"

"I never saw such a girl. Scores of men have asked for her, but she's as stubborn as a mule. She declares that the only one she'll marry will know how to read and write, and will own books like the ones the judge has."

Saïd laughed. "Tell her tomorrow, 'Saïd now knows how to read and write, but he won't marry you—he'll marry a girl from Egypt!'"

"You'll marry an Egyptian?"

"A beautiful girl from Alexandria!" Saïd replied mischievously. And he went on to recount for her what he had heard from Mahmoud about the girl he was in love with. Then he added, "I used to pass beneath her window every day. She would be looking out bashfully and smiling. She was beautiful from afar, gorgeous from close up, and she improved with every glance. Her face was just like the full moon, and her smile—oh, if you could see her smile, Mother!"

Saïd was smiling, amused by his game, but his mother had stopped eating.

"You'll marry an Egyptian and live over there?"

"I'll live there and till the fields like the rest of the Egyptians."

This talk was unsettling for Amina, and she changed the subject. "Ammar asked me about you today. When will you go to see him?"

"I'll go tomorrow."

The following day, Saïd set off right away in the direction of the hill. He was climbing it when one of the guards blocked his way.

"Where to?" said the guard.

"I'm going to see Ammar, the Sultan's servant."

"Are you a stranger to the island?"

"I'm not a stranger here, I'm Saïd, son of Amina the baker."

"Since you're of the island, how is it you don't know that it's forbidden for men to climb the hill, where the prison cells are, and the high house in which the women's quarters are located, as well as the fortress of the Sultan himself?"

"But I want to see Ammar. I went away, and I was gone a long time. Ammar can no longer get down the hill, so there's no way for me to see him except to come up myself and visit him."

"Go back the way you came, man, and don't make trouble!"

Saïd turned to go back down, then headed toward the fishermen's beach. Hafez hadn't yet returned from his fishing expedition. He sat with some of the fishermen, helping them mend their nets. One of them laughed, impressed with how quickly he worked. "You haven't forgotten, Saïd!"

"No, I haven't forgotten."

They asked him about his journey. He told them, then asked them how things were on the island. They told him everything was just as it had been when he left: "The Sultan is in his castle; the slaves are on the plantations, and not a week goes by that one of their men isn't arrested and thrown into the dungeon. And we, as you see, are just as we ever were: we go out fishing and we come back; we give the Sultan his rightful portion and keep the rest. The only new thing on the island is that base that's been set up by the English army, but they keep to themselves in the eastern section of the island: they don't have anything to do with us, and we don't have anything to do with them."

Saïd stayed with the fishermen for a while, then left their company and walked eastward to have a look at the base they had told him about. He walked along, following the shoreline, until he saw some buildings constructed from stone of a leaden color. He hadn't yet approached them when his path was blocked by barbed wire with armed guards behind it. So he turned and headed back to the house.

In the evening, his mother busied herself preparing two fish for dinner. Saïd said, "I tried to climb the hill to visit Ammar, but they stopped me, and the guard said that men aren't allowed to go up there."

His mother laughed. "You've become a man, Saïd, and now they're afraid to let you near the harem!"

Saïd did not laugh. "But I want to see Ammar—how am I going to see him?"

Amina continued with her preparation of the fish. When they sat down to dinner, she said to him, "I'll tell you a way you'll be able to climb the hill without passing the high house or attracting the attention of the guards. Do you know Execution Square? At the western end of the island?"

"I know it."

"When the square is on your right, you'll find the trail on your left. It's a rough and twisting path, but it will get you there. When do you plan to go?"

"Tomorrow."

"I'll tell Ammar, so that he can wait for you at the end of the trail."

In the morning, Saïd set out for the path his mother had described to him. When he arrived at the square, he remembered it, although he hadn't been near it since he was eight years old. On that day, the proclamation went out across the island announcing that Prince Nuʿmaan had become sultan in place of his brother, Aliaddin, who had broken faith and forsaken the ties of blood. Saïd told his mother that he wanted to go to the square to see what the Sultan would do with his brother. She refused. "Anything you see there will frighten you and break your heart. Don't go." But he had not obeyed her. He had gone with Hafez, without her knowledge. They wanted to see the show.

Saïd and Hafez, along with the rest who had thronged to the occasion, saw the demented sultan as he was led, manacled and blindfolded, into the square. They saw the swordsman raise his arm and then bring down the sword upon the condemned man. And they saw the head fly into the air, fall to the ground, and roll like a stone. Then they heard the Sultan's guards raise their voices in a cheer.

Saïd had never returned to this end of the island after that, and he would never have thought to come near it, had his mother not described this route to the hill as the one that would take him to Ammar.

Saïd made his way up the winding path, until he saw Ammar standing and waiting for him. His body had become thin to the point of emaciation, although he still had his considerable height. Saïd embraced him, and his eyes glittered with tears as he took in the shining ebony face, the cottony hair, and the familiar expression in his eyes.

Ammar seated Saïd beside him and began asking him about his trip. He listened to his tale of Egypt and its people, who worked as farmers, and its leader Orabi, whom the English had exiled after they crushed his army and defeated him. Ammar listened, his gaze alert, following the narrative with the expressions on his face, which kept the pace, whether swift or slow; he smiled or laughed, or his features clouded over with sadness, as Saïd recounted the story. It wasn't only Ammar's tongue that could tell stories: it was his face and his eyes, like an enchanted mirror that brought words to life, released them, and exposed that which was concealed within them, whether sorrow or joy, fear or hope.

When the sun was near to setting, Saïd rose to go back to the house. Ammar, reaching into his pocket, said to him, "I've brought you a gift."

Saïd laughed. "A piece of sugar, right?"

Ammar laughed, too. "You've outgrown pieces of sugar, Saïd." He drew his hand out of his pocket, opened it, and there in his palm was a golden dinar. "Sultan Khalid, may he rest in peace, gave this to me when his elder son, Aliaddin, got married. You hadn't been born yet, Saïd, nor had even your mother come into this world." He held out his hand with the dinar. "Take it, Saïd, take it as a dowry for your bride!"

CHAPTER SEVEN

Forbidden Coffee

ʂᴏᴄ꒰

Amina stood before the house, keeping watch over the road. What if a passerby should happen along and recognize the scent, or what if they were surprised by a visitor, who would then see with his own eyes Saïd and Hafez consuming a substance that the Sultan had forbidden?

Saïd had brought it when he returned from his travels. When he opened the bag and she saw the greenish beans it contained, she didn't understand what they were, so she asked him. "Coffee," he said.

"Coffee!"

"That's right."

"But it's forbidden!"

"Forbidden by whom?"

"The judge made the decree. He said it was a novelty, that all novelty is error, and that all error is from the devil. He issued the proclamation to the island that coffee was forbidden by order of the Sultan, because it is of the same nature as wine—an intoxicant and a poison that plays with the mind—and that anyone partaking of it was to be punished with one hundred lashes."

"But it's not a sin—in Egypt they drink it, and in Yemen they grow and sell it. No one has forbidden it except the Sultan of our island."

He paid no attention to what she told him. He roasted the coffee beans and ground them, then invited Hafez. They lit a fire, filled the long-handled pot with water, and gradually added the grounds. They sat and talked, waiting for the liquid to boil, while the pungent fragrance permeated the air all around them.

Amina wasn't happy with the situation, but she told herself patience was a virtue, and that two *rotls* of coffee wouldn't last forever. One day soon the fabric bag would be empty; she would wash it, dry it, and use it to store flour or dates, and then her mind would be at ease.

The bag was not empty when Umm Latif summoned her and took her aside, a little way from the kitchen courtyard, and whispered, "How is Saïd?"

"He's fine, praise God."

"Is it true that he drinks coffee?"

"*Coffee?* We didn't know the word until the proclamation went out that the Sultan had forbidden it. Saïd has never tasted it in his life, or seen what it looks like—he wouldn't recognize it if he did see it."

"Don't try to hide anything from me, Amina. Hafez is my sister's son, and I care for him just as you care for Saïd. My sister confided in me about what they were up to. She said, 'Saïd and Hafez are drinking coffee and going under cover of night to the slave plantations—it could be they're after some of the girls there.'"

"Umm Latif, we haven't allowed coffee into our house, and Saïd hasn't tasted it, nor does he go at night to the slave plantations. He goes to sleep before I do, and I wake up before he does. When I get up at night, I find him deeply asleep, so I pull the covers around him and go back to sleep."

"But Saïd and Hafez are inseparable friends: whatever one of them does, the other does, too!"

Amina left Umm Latif to get on with the baking, but the color had drained from her face—what if the rumor got out around the island that her son was indulging in coffee, and the news reached the Sultan?

And what if Umm Latif had spoken the truth, and Saïd was breaking the law, going in secret to the plantations to mingle with the slaves? Would he be going there just to keep company with them, or to lie with their women? Was it possible Saïd was doing that? Had the journey altered him, had he returned a reckless fool, with Hafez now following his lead and doing as he did; or was Hafez the one who had pressured Saïd into committing such follies?

Amina finished her work and left the kitchen courtyard, heading for home. She saw Ammar sitting in the shade of a tree, his eyes wet with tears.

"What's wrong, Ammar?"

"Nothing, Amina."

"But have you been crying?"

"I took a nap, then the cry of a dove woke me, and I wept. Do you like doves, Amina?" He didn't wait for an answer. "Did you tell me that Saïd had learned to write?"

"He has learned, Ammar."

"I want him to write a letter for me."

"A letter?"

"I'll buy a carrier pigeon and give it a letter to carry to my mother."

"In what country, Ammar?"

"The pigeon will know its way. Tell Saïd that I want him to write a letter for me."

"I'll let him know, Ammar, but I want to complain to you about him." She sat down beside Ammar, feeling relieved at having found someone to whom she could unburden herself.

"Saïd drinks coffee, Ammar."

"Coffee!"

"He drinks coffee and goes to the plantations that we are forbidden to enter."

"Don't worry, Amina. He's a young man. Soon enough he'll settle down and be sensible."

"If the Sultan found out about this business of drinking coffee, he would order Saïd to be flogged a hundred lashes, and he might throw him in the dungeon. And if anyone informed on him about the visits to the plantations, God knows what his punishment might be."

"I'll speak to him, Amina. Send him to me, and don't forget to tell him to get a pen and paper so that he can write a letter for me."

Amina departed, leaving Ammar seated beneath the tree thinking about the letter and the carrier pigeon and the things Saïd had been up to. "Youth has its follies," Ammar thought to himself. When he was Saïd's age, a friend of his had stolen a bottle of wine from one of the princes, and they had drunk it together. The fieriness of it was strange at first, then appealing, and then it spread all through the body and warmed the heart. They drank, and laughed, enjoying their conversation and the trick they had played on the prince. They kept on drinking until their heads grew heavy. Ammar's companion fell asleep, but Ammar wept as if all his cares had crowded in on him at once. Did coffee, then, like wine, stir up the heart and conquer the soul? He had never drunk coffee in his life, had never even heard of it until the Sultan's proclamation went out saying that it was forbidden.

And the Sultan had forbidden him to marry Maliha. If Ammar could have followed his own inclination, he would have climbed the highest minaret on the island and announced that Nuʿmaan was an ungrateful dog. But he suppressed what was in his heart, concealing it from others so long as the Sultan was Sultan, and he a slave whose own soul didn't even belong to him. He smiled at the Sultan, bathed him in rose water, and put on his slippers for him, wishing all the while that he could see him tied to a stake—now *that* would really bring a smile to his face. Nu'maan was an ungrateful dog, but the dove was a righteous bird, one that would befriend a stranger and chase off his loneliness. The dove sang to her mate, flying wherever he flew and landing where he landed, and if the mate should be lost, then the dove remained alone, like that dove in the tree whose cries had made him weep.

That evening Amina told Saïd what Umm Latif had said to her. He replied, "I went only twice to the plantations. Hafez brought me along with him to visit some of the slaves who are around our age—he got to know them when his job was to deliver fish to the princes' houses at the plantations. We sat, we had a good time with them, and we went home. That's all there is to it."

"This is no explanation, my son. The Sultan has forbidden us to enter the plantations. You know that if anyone informed on you, you would be severely punished. Socialize as much as you like with the fishermen, but there's no good reason to take chances."

"Don't worry, Mother—I won't go anymore."

Then he told her that the captain of the boat on which Hafez worked had agreed that Saïd might work with them. "Starting tomorrow, I'll go out fishing with them."

"Why don't you work as a porter at the harbor?"

"I like going to sea, Mother."

It was as if he had heard the words from his father, and was repeating them. The same voice, the same manner of speaking. It was as if he was Abdullah, her husband, and time had turned back twenty years. "The sea is beautiful and wide, like the mercy of God. The sea is our father, Amina, and its goodness is limitless."

"But it kills, Abdullah."

"Don't blaspheme against God's blessings, Amina. The earth also kills."

The sea had taken him, but his son and his voice remained.

She gazed at Saïd while he slept. In his physique and the composition of his face he most resembled his grandfather, her own father: tall and strongly built, with well-defined features, brown skin, a clear complexion, green eyes, and chestnut hair that was thick and coarse. The look in his eyes, though, he had taken not from his grandfather but from the milk of her breasts, when she was in mourning and suckling him: an expression of quiet but abiding and reproachful sorrow, which imbued his features with the poignancy of an orphaned child, even in his manhood.

Tomorrow he would go out fishing. Would the sea deal with him as it had dealt with his father and his grandfather? Men loved the sea. They went to it with longing, like lovers. What was it, then, that they loved about it, when between their two hands was the earth, whose water was fresh and cold? The earth was more generous: you sowed it with seed and it gave you its crops and its fruits in full measure, so why did men love the sea?

"The sea is good, the sea is generous," repeated Amina, speaking out loud, fearful of the sea's rancor and thinking to appease it. "Saïd is in your hands, sea, so look after him and each time he goes out to you, bring him back safely to me."

Amina slept, still on her tongue the murmured incantations meant to win over the sea with praise and thanks. But in a dream she saw an orchard of banana and lemon trees, and a clothesline on which hung infants' diapers and tiny clothes. She was sitting at the edge of the orchard turning a quern and milling wheat. She told Saïd about her dream as he was preparing to go out in the predawn twilight, but he just laughed, picked up his bundle of provisions, and set out.

CHAPTER EIGHT

The Locked Vault

𝕊𝕆ℝ

The Sultan spent a long time relieving himself in the bathroom. He disliked the castor oil that had been prescribed for him, so he traded one irritation for another, suffering stomach pains throughout the day, which were punctuated by trips to the bathroom. He went to the lavatory time after time, no matter how painful or protracted the discomfort, rather than endure that single unpleasant moment in the morning.

The Sultan would crouch there trying to relieve himself, thinking all the while that he alone was envied by the envious masses, who had no idea of the enormity of the responsibilities that rested upon his shoulders.

In his youth, he could kindle a blaze in his heart by opening up his vaults and running his hands over the rare and precious jewels. Then he abandoned this habit, with the exception of one vault, which he continued to open every day, to gaze for a while at what was kept there.

A man grows up, is hardened by experience, and learns to trust no one, not wife, brothers, or children. Bint al-Mohsen was an old woman, gray-haired, empty-headed, concerned with nothing except depriving him of what God had made lawfully his, and machinating against the women he took as concubines, as if he was committing adultery with them. His sons were imbeciles, with brains like worn-out sieves, and the only one among them worthy to be his regent had returned from the land of the English like a viper that had changed its skin. He had come to him bareheaded, leading behind him an emaciated she-goat and declaring that he had married her. So he dismissed him from the court and, in his agitated fury, all but summoned the executioner to cut off his head.

But Mohammed insisted on a meeting with him, so he said to himself that the boy must have realized his offense, repented of his behavior, and come to ask for forgiveness and reconciliation. But the dog appeared before him dressed like an Englishman, wearing tailored trousers—scandalously form-fitting—and saying that he had come to discuss a plan for the development and advancement of the island "so it could be on a par with other nations, become a rising star, be illuminated."

"I've written everything down in these pages and brought them for you to read closely and consider the details."

"Summarize your plan in a sentence or two; as for the papers, I'll read them later."

"I suggest we set up a consultative council, and executive ministries; that we separate the state treasuries from your private ones; that we emancipate the slaves and have them work for wages; and furthermore . . ."

He stopped him in mid-sentence, for matters had become plain enough. Mohammed had come back from the land of the English to subvert the system of government on the island and impose constraints on his father the Sultan. The Sultan didn't need to read the papers or to know anything more. He summoned his guards and ordered them to arrest Mohammed and throw him in the dungeon. Then he ordered the deportation of that skinny goat of his on the next departing ship.

Soon afterward Bint al-Mohsen came to him to intercede for the Englishwoman, saying that she was expecting a child. "Our sons," he replied, "do not marry the daughters of the English. So let her go and take what's in her womb with her, for it has nothing to do with us."

Bint al-Mohsen pleaded with him, saying, "Wait until she delivers her child. I'll take it and raise it, and then you can deport her as you please."

Bint al-Mohsen had become unbalanced, lost her head—what could she want with a leprous child whose mother was a Christian? He dismissed her from his court and ordered the deportation of the Englishwoman.

The Sultan relaxed after relieving himself, clapping for his servants to bathe him and dress him in his robes. When they had finished, he looked at himself in the mirror, scrutinizing his image: a brilliantly white *jilbaab*; over that a camel hair *abaya* embroidered with gold thread; at his waist an ornamented belt in which was a dagger whose handle, fashioned from pure gold, appeared above his waist while its scabbard, inlaid with the costliest of gems, extended below it. The brown face was set in an expression of resoluteness, the eyes were alert; there was strength in the body, which was moderately tall; and in the clothing there was dignity. He adjusted the position of his turban, stroked his carefully cultivated beard, and smiled at the mirror, murmuring, "That is how an Arab Sultan should look!"

He had an appointment with Captain Smith, the head of the military base. Had the English officer requested this interview in order to intercede for Mohammed and his wife? If that was the case, then the secret would be out, manifest and clear, that the plan Mohammed had proposed was not one he had devised on his own, but rather the English had pressed him to it, and gotten his hopes up. If Smith brought up the matter, he would answer him as brusquely as possible, and inform him that he would not accept their interference in his family affairs.

But the captain had come for a different purpose. He told him that they had "near certain" information that some sort of action against him was being organized at the plantations.

"Do you mean to say that my sons, the princes, are conspiring against me?"

"No, I'm talking about the slaves. Ever since we arrived on the island, we've been aware of rumblings from the plantations, so we pursued the matter, keeping an eye out, until at last we determined that there were suspicious communications passing among the slaves, and indeed organized groups meeting at regular intervals. The name 'Siraaj' was repeated. We don't know to whom it refers, but we are convinced that these communications constitute a security threat to the island and to your personal safety. We wanted to bring you the evidence that has been furnished to us, so that you could confront the situation in a suitable way. We are ready to offer our assistance, if you ask it of us."

The Sultan conducted the English officer to the castle gate, and shook his hand in gratitude and thanks. Then he sent a messenger to the princes on the plantations, saying that they should come to him before the afternoon prayer. He also ordered his scouts and spies to attend a meeting: "Those at the plantations, and those at the port, as well as those who live in the tradesmen's quarter, and among the fishermen's and divers' huts: I want all of them, tonight, after the evening prayer."

Should he believe what Smith had conveyed to him? He must make sure. The English might be trying to beguile him with flattery and pretenses of friendship, concocting this whole idea in order to assist Mohammed, so that what he had suggested would seem like a necessity, inevitable, so long as the Sultan's rule was threatened, his defensive system ineffective. And if he believed the officer, what then? What was to be done?

The Sultan's meeting with the princes was stormy. He told them they were men of straw, unreliable, negligent and careless, fit only for the indolence of the women's quarters. "The roof is crumbling and threatening to collapse upon our heads," he said, adding, "This island is my property, and its bounties come out of my own funds. I delegated you to maintain security for me, but you neglected your duties, so the slaves have flouted your authority and made fools of you. I swear to the greatest, the most high God, if you don't change your ways, I'll throw you into the dungeon with Mohammed!"

He was furious, his face flaming with the wrath he turned on them. The effect on the princes was such that they skulked out, one after the other, not one of them daring to approach and kiss his hands.

After that the Sultan met with his scouts and spies. His anger had dissipated, the flame in his heart had been extinguished, and he had become cold as lead. He informed them in a calm voice, "I want precise intelligence, or else I shall cut off your heads, every one of you, without exception."

Not until very late at night did the Sultan retire. It was anxiety rather than anger that possessed him now, a choking oppressiveness, as if the air around him was made of iron. Ingratitude, that's what it was. It clotted the space around him, constricted his breathing, and weighed on his chest. Bint al-Mohsen, his sons, and his slaves: the whole lot of them were eaten up by envy—it had blinded them and rotted out their hearts, so that nothing remained but the ashes of ingratitude and bitter rancor.

He gave freely, yet nothing but ingratitude did he get for his munificence. Each time he was notified that a son had been born, he opened his heart and had his slaves bring gifts to the child and its mother; he even went himself to the mother and held the newborn in his arms, feeling how tiny, helpless, and vulnerable it was, and spread over it the wing of his compassion. He had given the seed of their existence, the flesh on their bones, their name, their wealth, and their position. And what had they given him in return?

It was said that the Sultan had fifty-seven sons. He was envied for having sired so many boys—and it had come to nothing . . . worse than nothing, for who could tell? Perhaps all of them were like Mohammed, concealing in their hearts a speckled adder, awaiting its chance to deploy its venom.

His mouth was bitter, his heart heavy, and there was no one but God to whom he might complain—and yet God knew . . . God knew how good and generous, how ill-used he was. Tears welled up in his eyes; he was overcome with loneliness and self-pity.

He went into his chamber to sleep, and was startled to find there a woman from among his slave girls. Preoccupied with his troubles, he had forgotten that it was Thursday night. He gazed at the slave girl. She was a young girl of slender build, with a face as lovely as the dawn. He approached her, glad that the conclusion of his wretched day should be graced by the companionship of this moon,[1] who had the fragrance of musk and the limpid gaze of a gazelle.

The Sultan sat beside her, feeling an urgent desire to talk to her, to unburden himself to her of all that was on his mind. He needed her sympathy; he wanted her to pity him, weep for him, and stroke his brow to comfort him. He held out his hand to her and smiled. She smiled. Why did she smile? Doubt and anxiety seized him at once. What if she was hiding a dagger, or some poison? What if she was in league with the slaves or the English or the princes or Bint al-Mohsen? What if she was after a piece of his hair or his clothing in order to perform some sorcery against him, to render him impotent or incapable of ruling the island? She was smiling strangely. He sent her away and went out onto the balcony. Perhaps the sea air would relieve his sense that he was strangling.

He left the balcony and rapidly descended the castle stairs, heading for the horses' stables. The guards leaped hastily to attention, raising their hands in a salute to the Sultan. He shouted at them, "Saddle up Flood!" They brought him his black stallion. He mounted it and rode away.

Mounting a horse was more pleasurable than mounting women. Raising horses was more useful than raising children. And Flood had never let him down as his children had done. The Sultan stroked the black stallion's neck. He had witnessed the horse's birth, had seen the black foal with its small white blaze, a little bird-shape that flowed from its forehead and gave a fine definition to the space between its eyes. "I name him 'Flood,'" he said. And Flood had not let him down. He had grown to live up to his name: fleet-footed and swift, if you spurred him he would fly. Horses didn't demand possessions. Behind their gentle eyes were hidden no hearts black with hatred and envy. As the Sultan stroked his horse's neck, it began to pace gently over the ground, swaying rhythmically with small steps, as if it could sense what was on its master's mind and was sympathizing with him. The Sultan told Flood everything that was on his mind. He talked, and wept, and was relieved and comforted. Feeling better, he spurred his horse vigorously with his knees. The horse took off at a gallop, pelting the earth firmly with its hooves.

Some days later the Sultan received written reports from the princes and verbal ones from the scouts and spies. The princes asserted that the situation at the plantations was stable and systems were operating normally there. They said that after an investigative probe they had found nothing to arouse any doubt or suspicion. But the spies told a different story. One of them assailed him with the news that a group of young slaves known for their grousing sat up late together each night. Another came to him with information on some sailors who sneaked out at night to go to the plantations and buy vegetables and fruits from the slaves, which they smuggled back to their houses under cover of darkness. And a third provided him with the name of someone who had publicly reviled the Sultan, as well as the names of three slaves who met secretly with their brothers who worked at the English base, despite the prohibition against contact between the base and the residents of the island. Five of the spies were united in their declaration that there was no man anywhere on the plantations who was called "Siraaj"; but there was an elderly woman who bore that name.

After the Sultan had gone over the reports he received, he issued orders that the three princes who supervised the plantations be replaced by some of his other sons who were of age. He designated them by name. And he ordered the arrest of those who were under suspicion. Whoever spoke ill of him or plotted against him would have his tongue and his genitals cut off. Anyone who stole would have his hand lopped off; and anyone who defied one of the Sultan's commands would receive a public flogging of one hundred lashes.

The Sultan was convinced that prevention was better than a cure, and that the punishment of every suspect was a guaranteed deterrent to others, who would then think twice before committing any reckless act, even if it was only sneaking off with a dozen lemons in the dark. As for the woman called Siraaj, her case perplexed him, for the island had no women's prison, and the long-standing customs and traditions established with regard to women prohibited their execution or public flogging. Should he let her be? And if she were a dangerous type, a threat to the island and its security? Should he order her eyes to be put out, her teeth extracted, and her nose cut off, to serve as a warning to others? The matter confounded him, so he ordered her to be brought to him, so that he could see her, interrogate her, and ascertain just what there was to her.

They brought her, and his chamberlain informed him of the fact. The Sultan said, "Let her come in." Two of the guards entered with a large basket between them, each man grasping a handle. He didn't understand the meaning of what he saw, until he realized, as the guards set the basket down on the floor, that the woman was inside it. Were they mocking him? Had he become a bad joke? And who would dare to make a mockery of the Sultan? She was a skinny old woman, lame, half-blind, and toothless, with thinning hair, resembling a dried-up, lifeless stick of firewood.

"Are you Siraaj?"

"Are you the Sultan?"

God in Heaven. The broken-down old crone didn't answer the Sultan's question, but questioned him herself, as if she was the interrogator!

"Aren't you Sultan Khalid?"

"Sultan Khalid?"

"It's you, the very one. Did you think I wouldn't know you? I danced and sang at the circumcision of your son Aliaddin until my midsection ached and my voice grew hoarse. How old is Aliaddin now?"

It was not only the woman's body that had shriveled up like dried fruit, but her mind had decayed as well, and left her empty of reason and memory. Nevertheless, something seemed to be going on in her head. The woman huddled in the basket, casting her eyes from the ceiling of the hall to the floor, staring befuddled at the chandeliers, the carpets, and the servants, muttering over and over to herself, "It's Leilat-al-qadr[2] and its power has opened itself up to you, Siraaj, so ask for what you will.

"Oh, Sultan, I have three requests, no more: I want a husband, because my husband died. I want a ewe, because I sold my ewe when I was beset by hardships. And I want a house, because my son's wife treats me very badly. Is this too much to ask?"

The Sultan smiled. Then his smile widened and he began to laugh aloud, until he all but fell over backward from laughing so hard. Then he summoned his guards, who picked up the basket and left, while the woman shouted hoarsely, "Isn't this Leilat-al-qadr? Isn't this the Sultan Khalid? What happened?"

CHAPTER NINE

The Festival

ഇറ

Tonight the island was sparkling with festival lights, which dazzled the eyes, and kindled the rage of the envious. The Sultan smiled to himself as he reclined lazily in the bathtub, with his personal servant soaping his head and body for him.

He had invited the consuls and vice-consuls and those of highest rank from the neighboring islands, and ordered the distribution of ornaments and lights, and he spread tables of food for all the residents of the island. Thus from near and far, one and all—both those whose hearts were kindled with good will and those heated by the embers of hatred—would know that the strong and far-reaching hand of Nu'maan bin Khalid was extended, bestowing limitless abundance.

He would sit on the high dais, surrounded by his guests and the members of his household. Horses would dance to the pulse of the *mizmars* and the drums, race camels would run, snake charmers would display their arts, and the people would see the rarest of the wondrous animals and birds in his possession. At nightfall, there would be fireworks to disperse the evening shadows with their luminous colors.

The servant poured rose water over the Sultan's head and body, after which another servant, who had been standing at the ready, wrapped the Sultan in a large towel and dried him. Then a third servant took over, dressing the Sultan in his *jilbaab* and *abaya*, slippers, belt, and finally his turban. The Sultan gazed at himself in the mirror. A sense of profound well-being filled him. He smiled, then sent for Bint al-Mohsen.

She appeared before him in a flowing black robe with gold threads woven into its fabric, and a swatch of cloth sewn with rows of gold coins covering her face from the tip of the nose to the neck. Nothing of the wrinkled face or the ancient body showed. The Sultan smiled. "The scheming old hag! She's completely covered except for her kohl-lined eyes, her gangling height, and the crown of her head!" He nodded his head in approval and dismissed her.

He summoned the rest of his harem. A multitude of women came before him, painting the hall with the radiant colors of their clothing. He cast his gaze about, inspecting them. Their hair was veiled, their faces screened, and their bodies chastely covered. Only their eyes bore witness that the Sultan's flock was graced by the loveliest gazelles. He murmured his satisfaction and dismissed them.

In Execution Square (on this day, Festival Square), the people who had come out early saw the high dais erected for the Sultan to sit on, and they saw the waiting guards standing at attention, with ammunition belts crossed upon their chests.

Hafez said, "Let's go and see the beasts of prey that are being displayed in cages."

Amina replied, "The beasts of prey won't fly away—let's see the snake charmers first."

"What's the fun in watching snake charmers? Let's go, Saïd."

The two boys left Amina and Tawaddud standing bemused before one of the snake charmers, wondering how he could make a viper emerge from an empty basket, then get it to go back in, then turn over the basket and—presto!—the basket would be empty once more.

Saïd and Hafez plowed through the crowd in the opposite direction, away from the square and toward where the caged beasts were. The hyena was the first thing they saw: a small-chested animal with a protruding belly and large haunches and rump. Saïd asked Hafez, "Why do they say 'foolish as a hyena'?"

"I don't know. I only know that hyenas dig up graves and eat corpses."

They took in its appearance, its monotonous pacing in the cage, and its limping steps. Then they turned away from it.

They looked at the lion, impressed by its massive frame, its regal bearing as it sat there, and the thick mane that encircled its head. The hyena seemed pitiful to them now, as they stared at this awesome, brawny creature, beautiful in spite of its glowering face. All at once it roared loudly. The boys laughed aloud even as they felt their guts convulse with alarm—a feeling between terror and a thrilling warmth. The lion roared twice, then rose to its feet. The boys stood transfixed.

If anyone had told them that there was in the world an animal more beautiful than the lion, they'd have called him a liar, but no sooner did they move to the third cage than their own eyes made liars of them. They stared, breathless, their feet fastened to the ground as if they had been nailed there. The beast that was before them was more majestic than the lion, surpassing him in its magnificence. Its body was like the lion's, its chest, haunches, and rump huge, taut and muscular, but it was longer and more graceful, and its lustrous gold pelt was shot through with black stripes. There was a subtle quivering in its motionless face, and its eyes glittered like night stars, despite the glaring sunlight. It was as strong as the lion, and as regal, but it trod the earth in a sauntering gait with the lightness and suppleness of a cat.

Hafez said suddenly, "Let's climb the hill and go get Ammar."

They began the ascent in silence. They were thinking about the third and last beast they had looked at, recalling the particulars of its image, and wondering about it. What could it be, and where was it from? How could a hunter have been able to catch it? Did he throw his nets over it? How was it that it didn't shred them? Did he wound it with a gun, and if so, then where had that magnificent body, with its haughty stride, been struck? And how could that enormous frame tread upon the earth with such lightness and grace? How did it look, they wondered, when it ran? How did it look when it jumped? How did it look riled up and ferocious? Preoccupied with these questions, they kept quiet until they reached the top of the hill.

They encountered some difficulty in persuading Ammar to go down with them. "First of all, we want you to see the beasts of prey that we saw, and second, there's a surprise we've prepared for you."

Ammar stared at them, puzzled. "A surprise?" The boys exchanged a mischievous smile, but they didn't reveal the secret to him.

Ammar leaned one arm on Saïd's shoulder and the other on Hafez's. He wanted to walk with their assistance, but they encircled his waist each with one arm, and walked without his feet touching the ground until they had descended the hill.

Ammar recognized the beast, and told Saïd and Hafez that it was called a "tiger."

"Two years ago it was as small as a puppy. The Sultan used to put a collar around its neck and hold the end of its chain in his hand."

Speaking confidently, as if the tiger was his, or as if he had a special relationship with it, Hafez said, "Now the tiger has grown, and the Sultan doesn't dare collar it or hold the end of its chain in his hand!"

Startled, Ammar looked at Hafez, then turned his eyes upon the tiger. He saw that there it was, alone in its cage, and yet the Sultan didn't "dare." He laughed, delighted with Hafez's words and with the idea.

"Now we'll take you to the 'surprise'!"

℀   ℀   ℀

The Sultan entered the square at the head of a procession as the drums beat, the music played, necks were craned, and those who were still far off hastened to find places closer in, from which they would be able to see.

Amina was settled upon the ground in front of a fortune-teller. She whispered to the seashells and returned them to the woman, who manipulated them in her hands, threw them onto the sand, and stared at them. Then she gathered them up quickly and thrust them into her handkerchief. She returned to Amina the two dates that she had pressed upon her in payment. Retreating hastily, the woman said, "I'm going to watch the Sultan."

As they made their way to where they could watch the goings-on, Amina said to Tawaddud, "Do you think the fortune-teller saw something that boded ill for me, and hid it from me?"

Tawaddud replied, "You have this habit, Amina, of seeing an evil omen in a passing bird. The woman ran off so that she wouldn't miss the spectacle of the Sultan and his guests and his women's clothes and jewelry." Tawaddud repeated this opinion several times, but all the same Amina could not dispel her sense of foreboding, even when the cannon's roar signaled the beginning of the fireworks display, the likes of which the islanders had never seen before. Clusters of brilliant light unfurled into space, painting its blackness now with green, now red, now yellow. Amina watched and listened with a distracted mind, wondering: What on earth had the fortune-teller seen that her conscience had not permitted her to divulge?

℀   ℀   ℀

Ammar discovered what the surprise was. The younger slaves were putting on a festival within the festival. The princes were keeping company with the Sultan, and what with the uproar in Execution Square, the secret drums in the unfrequented clearing in the midst of the palm groves would go unnoticed.

65

Ammar saw that the slaves had spread themselves out on the ground in a wide circle around the clearing, and he saw heaps of firewood underneath small pots. Saïd told him they were coffee pots, and it was then Ammar realized that the strange, distinctive fragrance with which the place was permeated was the smell of coffee.

"Have some, Grandfather."

"Thank you, son."

Ammar spoke with a smile, then began to sip the coffee, tasting it wonderingly.

The drummer began to beat his instrument, signaling for the party to begin. The center of the clearing was empty but for a tall palm tree in one section of it. At the foot of the palm stood a masked man who was elevated on two tall wooden stilts.

Loud and rapid drumbeats were followed by slow, distinct taps, to whose rhythm the man on stilts moved forward, out of the shadow of the palm tree and into the center of the clearing. When he reached the middle, he spread his arms and began swaying right and left, circling, turning, bending, standing up straight, all to the accompaniment of the beat of the drum. Then another dancer entered the clearing and began following the first, imitating every movement he made. Against the masked dancer's exaggerated height and his outspread arms, the second dancer looked as though he was merely a shadow cast upon the ground by the first.

They danced on, in harmonious concord, until the drum sounded with a series of rapid beats, at which the man on stilts began to spin around quickly without stopping, while the small dancer duplicated his movements. Then the taller gave the shorter one a knotted handkerchief and withdrew, returning to the shade of the palm tree.

Hafez leaned toward Ammar and whispered, "This man is the spirit of the tree—did you recognize him?"

Ammar stared at him uncomprehendingly, saying nothing. Then all at once the light broke, as if a great window had opened on the sunrise, and he saw everything. His face lit up, and he bent toward Hafez. "It's the spirit of the tree," he said. "I've recognized him, I know him. And the knotted handkerchief contains the sap, doesn't it?"

Hafez laughed. "See? You remember everything, Ammar!"

Ammar murmured, as if to himself, "Yes, I remember everything, I will remember everything."

It seemed he would weep with emotion; he was fighting back tears. He leaned toward Saïd and whispered to him in explanation,

66

"The man on stilts is the spirit of the tree, and this one who is running in fear now is carrying the sap in the knotted handkerchief. It's up to him to protect it."

He was holding the handkerchief and running about in the clearing, moving to the incessant drumbeat. He peered to the right and to the left, before him and behind him, an expression of fright and anxiety etched upon his face, until his fears took shape in another dancer who entered the clearing and began chasing him.

The new dancer wore a mask that expressed cruelty and wickedness: the eyes were empty, the mouth was twisted, and the eyebrows were two arches that met in an emphatic frown. The evil mask pursued the dancer until he caught up with him and undertook to block his way. The dancer threw up his arms in front of his face and dodged the other, still holding the handkerchief: when he bent his torso to the right, the other bent to the left, and the dance went on. The confrontation escalated with the accelerating drumbeat, until a new dancer stole into the clearing and stealthily approached the one with the knotted handkerchief, who surrendered it to him. He tied it around his neck and began waving his arms, driving off the evil mask. He continued his dance while other dancers poured into the clearing to take part, passing the knotted handkerchief from one to another and taking turns tying it around their necks.

To the rhythm of a powerful drumbeat, slow and regular, the dancers spread their arms in a deflecting motion, with which they faced down the evil mask. They were advancing on him as he fell back. Then the drumbeat rose in an accelerating crescendo, and the evil mask made off at a run.

The slaves poured into the center of the clearing and started a rowdy dance of release and intoxication. Saïd watched the whole thing, amazed and dazzled. He was even more amazed when Hafez leapt into the clearing and joined the slaves' dancing. He spread out his arms in front of him and moved his feet, shoulders, and haunches rhythmically to the beat of the drum. When and how had Hafez learned to dance that way?

Ammar leaned over and shouted in his ear, "If I were younger, I'd join the dance. Why don't you join in?"

Saïd felt the blood rise to his face and he muttered, embarrassed, "I don't know how."

CHAPTER TEN

Saïd's Dream

ℰↃᏟᎡ

Saïd felt as though he was choking, as the man who rode upon his shoulders wrapped his legs around his neck and exerted pressure, insulting him and beating him. The man, who had hooves like a horse or a donkey, began to urinate and defecate, and Saïd wished he might die. Then he woke up.

It was only a nightmare, but even so a feeling of uneasiness lingered, as if what happened in the dream was an ordeal he had lived; and he was unable to relieve himself of its pressure, even after he had escaped from it. It wasn't until a few days later that Saïd remembered that in the dream he had retrieved an episode from a story that Young Mahmoud had told him when they were wandering the streets of Alexandria.

Saïd went to the ocean, dragging his feet as if the oppressive burden he had carried on his shoulders in the dream had moved into his legs. He came back from fishing, still dragging his feet as he had done going out. But now he knew that the dread in his heart had been a presentiment of disaster that was concealed in daytime's creases and folds.

He told Amina what had happened. She wept, and cursed the ship's captain, who mistreated the fishermen and pushed them around. Then she wiped her tears with the palms of her hands and said, "But Umm Latif must be doing something to help Hafez, for he is her sister's son, and she's been attached to him since he was an infant in diapers. She won't let them throw him in the dungeon just because he insulted the captain of the ship or shoved him in a moment of anger. No doubt she'll go to Bint al-Mohsen and beg her to intercede for him with the Sultan. And who knows, perhaps God will soften Lady Alia's heart, out of compassion for Hafez's father and mother and sisters, whom he supports."

Saïd was pale, with a look of defeat in his eyes; Amina tried to soothe and reassure him. But when she extinguished the lamp and stretched out on her bed, she began to weep again, for she had known Hafez ever since he had tripped over his "R's," reversed the syllables of words, and glanced nervously around him as he walked, fearful of demons from the sea. She had fed him along with Saïd, dividing the one loaf of bread between the two of them, and she had run after them to discipline them when they misbehaved. She would get hold of one of them and spank him, and the two of them would be chastened, not only the one who had felt the sting of her hand, but also the one who hadn't. A clever and good-natured boy he was, and she had often teased him, saying, "If I had a daughter, Hafez, I'd marry her to you, even if you didn't find her attractive!"

Laughing, Hafez would retort, "I'd appeal to Ammar and say to him, 'You wouldn't make me marry Amina's ugly daughter, would you?'"

Amina wept silently, thinking that Saïd was deeply asleep.

But Saïd was lying awake like his mother, wondering whether he had failed his friend when he needed his help. "Was I wrong to obey the ship captain's order? Were we wrong—when he threatened us, tied Hafez up, and whipped him—to return so submissively to our work, with Hafez bound by a rope right before our eyes? But what else could we have done, when the captain had threatened us with the same fate if any of us dared to defy him and disobey his orders? And why did Hafez fly into such a rage that he grabbed the captain by the collar instead of just talking calmly to him and trying to make him see that the fisherman Maarouf wasn't feigning illness—he really was sick, and unable to go to work? Wouldn't it have been better for Maarouf to pull himself together and haul nets with the rest of us—since the captain was making an issue of it and was in no mood to give in—instead of letting the situation escalate into a fight?" Hafez had grabbed the captain's collar in Maarouf's defense, then had lost control and run over to one of the baskets of fish and hurled its contents into the sea, in rage and protest. "Did all that really have to happen?"

"Are you asleep, Amina?"

"I'm not asleep, Saïd."

"Did I fail Hafez?"

"It was out of your hands, Saïd . . . what could you have done?"

They fell silent again, as if they had dozed off, but neither Amina nor her son was capable of sleeping. Both were preoccupied with the same question: Saïd and Hafez had been friends since childhood, so how could one of them come to grief while the other stood by unable to help? This couldn't be . . . and yet what power, indeed, was within Saïd's grasp to put things right?

When Amina returned from her work the following day, she told Saïd about Umm Latif. "The poor thing came to the kitchen today with her eyes puffy from crying. Then she went to Bint al-Mohsen to try to win her sympathy. She said that Hafez had made a mistake, but that he was young and foolhardy. She said his father was blind and his mother ill, and that it was Hafez who was supporting his ten brothers and sisters. She pleaded with her and kissed her head and her hands, and entreated her by all that was dear to her to take pity and intercede with the Sultan on Hafez's behalf. She came back in a state worse than when she had gone. Bint al-Mohsen's answer was 'no.'"

Amina was in a rebellious rage, but she avoided letting Saïd know what was in her heart. After all, what if her feelings were transmitted to him, with the result that he committed some hasty act and met the same fate as his friend? She spent the night silently calling for God's vengeance upon the ship captain, the Sultan, and the Sultan's wife. "We serve them in miserable drudgery all day long so that they can fill their bellies. Then we go to them with a request whose fulfillment will cost them nothing but a word, a word that will bring us back to life, and they refuse it." This was what Tawaddud had said, and she was right. Was it possible that the sea was more generous than they were? Indeed it must be that the sea was more generous, for the sea had no heart or mind, nor had it been born of human flesh, such that we should reproach it and curse it and say to it, "Why have you no mercy on us, oh sea? Are you not human like us?"

           ℭ   ℭ   ℭ

"Who's knocking at this hour of the night?" Amina wondered, fearful of some evil chance, as she got up to open the door.

The visitor was a young black man, one of the plantation slaves. He asked after Saïd. She was going to pretend he wasn't there, but the visitor, as if he had read her mind, said, "Don't be afraid, Aunt. I mean no harm—I'm his friend."

She invited him in and woke Saïd. She stayed up, fighting off sleep until the stranger left, but just when she asked the reason for his visit, sleep overcame her. When she awoke in the morning, Saïd had gone out early to fish, so she didn't see him, but she saw the cloth bag filled with green coffee beans and knew that the nighttime visitor had brought it. She wondered, "How could a young plantation slave have gotten hold of coffee when it's grown in Aden?"

℘ ℘ ℘

"Will you drink some coffee with me?"

"Drink coffee? Me?"

"It's not a sin. Believe me, Mother, in Egypt they drink it, and in Yemen as well, and everywhere."

"Are you sure?"

"I'm sure—I swear."

"I'll taste it, then."

Diffidently, she took a sip of the coffee, marveling at the taste, which was strong and intense, like its fragrance. She took a second sip, and then a third, finding it pleasant despite the bitterness. She laughed with the gaiety of one abandoning herself to folly.

"If it's a sin, on your head be it!"

Saïd laughed, too. "It *must* be a sin, since it's made you laugh as if you'd drunk wine!"

Amina poured herself another measure of the coffee. Smiling, Saïd said, "Since you like it, I'll grow a coffee tree for you in the orchard you saw in your dream—what do you say?"

"And if the Sultan should find out?"

The Sultan didn't know that the slaves drank coffee, or that they cultivated the forbidden trees behind a screen of carob and tamarind trees, whose huge trunks and dense shade shielded the coffee trees and protected them from infestations of locusts, as well as from burning sun and prying eyes. The Sultan didn't know that his slaves drank coffee and were preparing to depose him. Hafez had told Saïd about this, and he had listened uneasily, for what recourse did powerless slaves have against a sultan who lived in a fortress defended by armed guards? A potent and vicious sultan, who cut off tongues and genitals, and cast people into the dungeon on the slightest suspicion: what would he do if this matter became known to him? He would reap a crop of heads as if they were stalks of corn at harvest time, and the blood would flow in rivers until it tinted the sea and dyed even the pearls nestled in their oysters.

That is what Saïd told Hafez, but his friend was unyielding. "All the same, we will try," he said, "and we might succeed. Are you with us?" Saïd didn't answer him. His tongue wouldn't obey him with a resolute and final "no," but reason held back the reckless "yes" that

71

might draw in its wake God alone knew what manner of catastrophe. He was still confused, poised between "yes" and "no," when the night visitor came to ask him about his decision. He came and went, and Saïd still kept turning the question over in his mind. The more he wrestled with it, the more he missed Hafez, and the more his absence pressed upon him and the more exhausted he was by his thoughts, turning around and around in his head like a solitary fishing boat caught in a whirlpool in the sea.

He went to see Ammar. "Have you come to write the letter for me, Saïd?" Ammar asked him.

"I haven't got hold of a pen and paper yet, Ammar."

"Don't forget about it, because I want the letter to arrive quickly. How are you, Saïd?"

"I'm troubled, Ammar. Ever since they took Hafez, I've been friendless, spending evenings by myself, and in the mornings I go to the fishing boat in a bad mood, because I can no longer stand the sight of the captain. I dreamed about him. I dreamed he was riding on my shoulders, and he was about to choke me, wrapping his legs around my neck."

"How strange!"

"The dream isn't strange, because Young Mahmoud told me the story of Sindbad the Sailor, who met a crippled old man and carried him, meaning to do a good deed. Then it became clear that the man was a devil with hooves, who kept tormenting him and beating him and forcing him to work, until Sindbad rid himself of it, threw it off his shoulders and beat it with a rock."

"How did Sindbad get rid of it if it was a devil?"

"He got a large fruit, removed its insides, and dried it. Then he filled it with grapes, and when they fermented he got the devil to drink the juice, and when it got drunk its limbs loosened, and Sindbad knocked it off his back and killed it."

"Did the man have the captain's face in your dream?"

"No, but it was a man with an ugly face, and he was tormenting me, so I knew it was the captain."

"It's not the ship captain you saw, Saïd; it's the Sultan—none other than the Sultan!"

Ammar had followed Saïd's narrative with a puzzled frown, but now as he spoke the creases in his forehead disappeared, and his features were restored to their usual sweetness, a smile spreading over his whole face.

"But you're mixing up the story and the dream, Ammar. In the story that Mahmoud told me, Sindbad killed the old man from the sea after he knocked him off his shoulders, but in the dream all I saw was myself with the man on my shoulders, beating me and almost choking me with his legs."

But for all that, Ammar insisted that Saïd's dream was a vision prophesying the downfall of the Sultan. At that moment, Saïd was on the point of unburdening himself to Ammar of everything that was on his mind. He was about to ask Ammar for advice, but he refrained, bade him good-bye, and went his way, wondering how his dream could have been a premonition of a favorable event that didn't occur in the dream. Should he go with the slaves and help them carry out the prophecy, or should he let reason prevail, seeing that everything around him confirmed that they were without recourse or power so long as the Sultan ruled with absolute authority?

Once again the whirlpool began to spin in his head, wearying him, just as Hafez's absence and the hateful ship captain's presence wearied him. Saïd sat down on the beach. The sky was clear, and studded with thousands of stars. He stared at it, remembering what Ammar had said to him when he was a small child: "These stars in the sky are the spirits of our loved ones who have gone before. Their fire is the torment of separation, and their light is the longing for meeting and reunion." Ammar told him that the sky was magnanimous and compassionate—it would not leave a person alone out in the open, but would shelter the stranger beneath its roof and ease his loneliness with its family of stars. If the stranger looked at them, he beheld them, but even if he walked with his eyes fixed upon the ground, still they would keep him company.

Would it be possible to find Mahmoud amongst all those stars? Saïd began casting his eyes from one star to another, saying, "This one is Mahmoud," then, "No, this one is not Mahmoud," and he would move to a different star and gaze intently at it. Just when Saïd was about to give himself up to despair and be on his way, he found him, and when he found him he wept until his tears mixed with the sea's mist upon his cheek.

CHAPTER ELEVEN

The Well-Kept Secret
೮ාౖය

Maliha had the power to predict sudden changes in the weather before they occurred. She would say that the following day there was to be a thunderstorm with a lot of rain, and indeed the next day there would be a thunderstorm and a downpour. Or she might say that there would be a raging sandstorm that would uproot trees and obscure the earth—and sure enough, in a matter of hours the sandstorm would engulf the eyes.

People would say, "How can it be that the weather was just clear, not a sign or portent that the eye could see?" They marveled, and Maliha marveled at their reaction, because the body could "see" more than the eyes could discern. Did not horses' bodies twitch with fright before a storm? Just so, her own body would be penetrated by excruciating pains that beat at her head like a blacksmith's hammer, or her joints would stiffen so that they felt like roots from which the water of life had dried up.

Amina strongly resembled her mother. Like her, she stood tall and straight, striking in appearance. The whiteness of her skin was slightly offset by a clear golden tint. Like her mother's, her hair was long and black, and she braided it into two plaits. But no one recognized in Amina, nor did she recognize in herself, that power her mother had, and therefore she was mystified by the certainty she found in her own heart that something was about to happen. She interrogated her heart: "What is it? Good or evil? Will you not explain, so long as you persist in your certainty?"

Amina decided to disregard her heart, and she carried on with daily life, sifting flour before sunrise, making dough and leaving it to rise. Then when the women began to crowd into the kitchen, she would commence rolling pieces of dough, laying them out, and placing them in the oven to bake. At night she would talk with Saïd and her eyes would well up with tears at the memory of Hafez. Then she would go to bed, her heart would tell her something was going to happen, and she would dismiss it.

On a certain night, Amina was not preoccupied with her heart's discourse, for she was thinking about what Tawaddud had whispered to her in the kitchen.

"And if Umm Latif should find out?" Amina had responded.

"She won't find out. And even if she does, she'll keep it to herself as if she hadn't heard."

"She's afraid, Tawaddud, and she's the manager of the kitchen. And if what we were doing should be exposed, they'd punish all of us, but her punishment would be more severe, because she's responsible for the provisioning of the kitchen and for what goes on there."

Tawaddud reassured her, and declared with conviction that Umm Latif was no impediment to what they were planning. "Leave it to me. If you agree, I'll see to everything."

Amina was about to repeat to Tawaddud what she had said before, the fears she had expressed, but instead she said, "See to it, Tawaddud, and may God shield us!"

Two days later, within earshot of all the women in the kitchen, Tawaddud said to Umm Latif, "By God, Umm Latif, Amina is more hard-pressed than all the rest of us. The baking she does on Thursdays is enough to exhaust ten women. Why don't you make a request to Bint al-Mohsen that she designate one or two women to help her?"

Umm Latif sighed. "I've asked her more than once, but she refused."

"And the solution to this problem?"

"The solution is in the hands of the One who solves all problems."

Tawaddud was silent, and went off to her work, as if convinced by Umm Latif's answer. The following day, she brought the subject up again. "An idea occurred to me, Umm Latif," she said. "Rather than go down the hill on Wednesday afternoons, only to climb back up it before dawn on Thursday, walking all that distance with a day of backbreaking labor in front of her, she could spend the night in the kitchen, get a full night's sleep, and have more time for the double shift of baking on Thursday."

One of the women cut into the discussion. "What's the matter with you, Tawaddud? You'll daub her eyes with kohl and blind her in the process.[1] What did Amina do to deserve to sleep alone here in this place, which is deserted at night? By God, even if they paid me all the money in the world, I wouldn't do it. I'd be afraid a ghost would come after me!"

Tawaddud laughed. "There aren't any ghosts, except human ones. In any case, I only wanted to help Amina, but if my idea doesn't suit her, never mind. Or, if she likes the idea but is afraid to sleep by herself, I'll stay with her, to entertain her and ease her loneliness. What do you think, Amina?"

Amina was staring at Tawaddud, amazed at the craftiness that had enabled her to put the question in a form that got her what she wanted. Umm Latif agreed to Tawaddud's proposal, which seemed to her and to all the women of the kitchen to be spontaneous, conceived on the spur of the moment; the suggestion that she stay in the kitchen with Amina on Wednesday nights seemed like an act of affection, sympathy, and friendship.

Amina was about to reveal the secret to Saïd, but she caught herself, remembering her promise to Tawaddud. So she hid away the secret as if it was locked in a box with an iron key, and carried on with her life. She climbed the hill in the predawn twilight and descended it as the sun was getting ready to set. Thus passed the five days after the plan was settled. Then on the sixth day, which was Wednesday, she went up and did her work, and as soon as day was done and the women had gone, she stayed behind with Tawaddud, talking with her as if the time before them was a paved path, and where it led or where it ended did not concern them, nor did they want from it anything but to wait by the side of the road until morning was upon them.

In this way it became the two women's habit, when night descended and the members of the high house were sunk in sleep, to roll up their sleeves and get to work. They would collect the dough that Amina had secreted away, over the course of seven days, to knead and bake. And as soon as the loaves were done, they would set to arranging them in two large baskets, into one of which they would insert the folded paper that Tawaddud had brought, hidden in her bosom. Then each of them would carry a basket on her head and they would proceed, under the cloak of night, to the predetermined place where they would meet the young man they recognized by his towering height, his limping gait, and his whispered utterance: "Good morning." They would answer in the same whispering voice, "Good morning to you." He would pick up the two baskets and take them away to smuggle them into the dungeon.

Amina and Tawaddud would go back the way they had come, two slender apparitions moving in the silent shadows, not exchanging a word until after they had made it to the safety of the kitchen. They would put on a pot of coffee, which would help them to continue their work in the morning that loomed, after they had spent the night without sleep. They would talk, speaking of various things, but neither one of them would refer to what they had undertaken, as if it hadn't happened, or it had been someone else's doing and they were unaware of it.

Amina did not tell Saïd her secret, nor did he tell her his, which was hidden by the broad leaves and dense roots of the banana trees. There he would meet with one of the young slaves. The slave would dictate a letter to Saïd, and Saïd would write it down in a precise, clear hand. The young man would fold it carefully and hide it, then carry it to one of the women slaves from the plantations, who in turn would convey it to Tawaddud.

Then Saïd went to see Ammar. He had decided to let him in on the affair. He told his comrade, "He may accept or he may refuse, but either way he'll still be Ammar, and he won't turn us in to anyone."

He came right out with what he had to say. "We're making preparations to overthrow the Sultan."

Ammar stared at him, and said nothing.

"You'll say it's rash conduct, and won't lead to anything but catastrophe, but we're making preparations to overthrow the Sultan, and God help us."

"You say 'we,' Saïd. Who's 'we'?"

"The plantation slaves and some of the fishermen."

"The slaves are planning to overthrow the Sultan?"

"Yes, and they want you with them."

Ammar gave a soft laugh, which came out almost like a moan. "And what does someone like me have to offer, a slave whose legs won't even carry him?"

"We want you to give us a description of the fortress from the inside: its halls, its corridors, its entrances and exits, the Sultan's bedchamber and his sitting room. Can you do that, Ammar?"

"This is a simple matter, Saïd, but will you storm the fortress? And how will you storm it, with armed guards at the gates?"

"We'll organize it, Ammar. All we ask of you is that you give us a description of the fortress from the inside, and the gates of the dungeon: how many there are, their positions, and the number of guards posted at each gate."

"Will you storm the dungeons as well?"

"Yes, that's what we'll do, Ammar."

"I can steal the keys to the dungeon for you."

Ammar spoke so calmly and confidently that Saïd wondered whether he was altogether clearheaded. "How?" he asked.

"The jailer is Marjaan, a skinny fellow who snores very loudly and tosses and turns a lot in his sleep. He sleeps in the same hall where I sleep."

"What does that have to do with the keys, Ammar?"

"He hangs the keys on a ring that's belted around his waist. When he goes to sleep, he takes off the key ring and puts it under his mat. As I told you, he tosses and turns a lot, which will make it easier to pull the key ring from under him, and since he snores, he won't notice even if I make the keys jangle as I'm pulling them."

"But others might notice."

"They do hard labor all day long, so they sleep like the dead at night."

"If they caught you stealing the keys, they'd inflict a severe punishment on you, Ammar—they might . . . they might even kill you."

"Don't be afraid, Saïd."

Ammar began to describe the fortress to Saïd. He got a tree branch and sketched in the sand. He drew the halls, the corridors, and the gates, and then he said, swishing the stick in his hand and erasing what he had drawn, "Repeat back to me what I said. Repeat it to me verbally first, and then repeat it as you draw in the sand, so I can be sure that it's fixed in your mind."

Saïd left him after they had settled on a meeting time for that night. "The ones who are working with us will be with me," he said. "We'll make an impression of the keys in wax, then return them so that you can put them back where they were."

Ammar stayed seated in his place. He wasn't calm now, as he had been when he was talking with Saïd. Rather, he felt himself growing fevered, his chest heaving, his breathing audible. Was this fear, or something akin to it? This was how he had felt on the day he found out that Maliha was in labor. He had run like a madman until he reached the fishermen's quarter. He had disappeared into the trees and sat waiting, while the sweat poured off him and his soul quivered as if it hung by a thread that swung him between life and death, until he saw them coming out of the house with the news. He wept then, and prayed to God. His prayer was like a Christian's, for he stayed unmoving in the place where he sat, because his body was so weak he hadn't the strength to get up and perform the prostrations.

When Saïd came and said, "We're making preparations to overthrow the Sultan," Ammar had listened calmly, as if it was ordinary news, or as if that ungrateful dog, with his slippers and his women and his fortress, was not crouched upon Ammar's chest—how could a man carry on his chest a fortress of iron and stone? And yet he did carry it on his chest, and he survived. And he loved Maliha, with her braided hair and her dimples; then Maliha was gone, and he survived.

The slaves wanted to overthrow the Sultan. Would God stand by their side? Would Ammar see himself, before he died, released from the imprisonment that had lasted almost a lifetime, or was it written in His book that the slaves were to live out their lives in torment on this earth, to be found wanting in the strength needed to free themselves? Would God bring them victory, or would He forsake them?

Ammar cried as he turned his face to God and uttered his prayers, and he continued to weep until he remembered Saïd's dream. He murmured then, "It's a sign." He wiped his tears and stood up, leaning on his cane. He headed toward the fortress, whose dark stone edifice appeared to him as a spectral presence, ephemeral as a bad dream. He repeated aloud to himself, "God will not desert us . . . it's not possible that He will desert us. Thank God I delayed buying the carrier pigeon. I'll wait until we've overthrown the Sultan, and then I'll write the letter to my mother and tell her about it."

CHAPTER TWELVE

The Lamp

ഇ)C♈

The secret was sinking in and leaving its impression: with the fishermen at sea, with the slaves on the plantations, with the sailors on their long journeys, in the memories of the old men sitting on their doorsteps, and with the women as they sang lullabies to their children.

The secret was sinking in, preserved in the people's hearts, locked up like the treasures of the wealthy, until the hour came when everyone turned his key in the lock, picked up his lamp in his right hand, and set out with the others.

Boys and girls, men and women, the elderly supported upon their canes or seated on litters borne by the able-bodied, infants at their mothers' breasts, plantation slaves, fishermen, sailors, pearl divers, carpenters, blacksmiths, and masons—all released their birds in the direction of the fortress and followed them, the lanterns in their hands.

Thousands of lanterns glowed in the darkness, blazing trails rugged and twisting, ascending. The guards in the highest towers saw them, and stared at them, and doubted their own eyes: lightning that blinded! Extraordinary lightning that cleaved the earth and not the sky! Lightning that traveled, climbing toward them. They were wondering among themselves, when the flocks of birds took them unawares. And they began to fire.

The people kept climbing until they reached the dungeon and applied the keys to the locks, shoulders to the gates, and axes to the walls. The dungeon opened up. They cheered, advanced, then drew back. Their eyes were engulfed in a darkness that carried the smell of the grave. The ancient dampness convulsed their guts.

Then, from the abyss of shadows, came the birds, rushing headlong as if they were blind, though they were not: slender, quivering birds, losing their feathers, but flying. The people's hearts were divided between terror and dread, and joyful exultation as they raised up their lanterns to form an arc of light for the men in the dungeon who surged forward behind the birds.

The people resumed the ascent, as large numbers of birds fell, tinged with the red of their own blood. The climbers knelt over them, picked them up to carry them on their heads, and kept going. Their enemy was before them: the Sultan in the fortress, and the guards with their ammunition on the walls. They advanced until, gathering their strength, they battered—with fists, with shoulders, with feet, with iron and wood and stone—the fortress of the Sultan.

Before them was their enemy, behind them their familiar, everyday sea—so how could this be? The enemy before them they confronted, and they had the power; the enemy behind them bombarded them from its battleships, and bodies fell, lanterns went out, fires ignited, surrounding life as it ran to try to preserve what life remained, until screams long-stifled filled the air, like the bursts of fire that punctured the darkness of night, each burst of light assailing the eyes of the people fleeing from death.

Why hadn't they reckoned on the English? Why had he not thought of it himself, and pointed out to them that the English would intervene to protect the Sultan? The question in Saïd's mind was a burning coal that tormented him as he ran in search of Ammar, among thousands of souls fleeing the bombardment. He must find Ammar, he must find him, lift him onto his shoulders, and carry him down the hill . . . and Amina . . . where . . . ? The question was unfinished as the missile caught him, and his body wavered, fell, along with the bird he had been carrying on his head.

క   క   క

Amina saw everything. The gravediggers as they wielded their pickaxes, piling up the dirt in heaps to either side, the hollow cleft in the belly of the earth. And the guards descending the hill, pushing in front of them the carts used for transporting dirt and slaughtered animals, piled with corpses.

Amina saw everything, as she sat in the shadow of a crucified man in whom she had discerned a resemblance to Saïd. It wasn't Saïd, she knew, but she sat without moving for three days and nights, until the guards brought down his body, and she took it from them.

She crouched upon the ground, formed a space between her thighs, and positioned her arms to enfold the body entirely. But her arms didn't reach, for the legs were crumpled and an arm dangled, so she bent her face and head and torso over him, to embrace the parts of him that overflowed.

ℰℛ   ℰℛ   ℰℛ

Amina keeps company with the stars. "Their light," Ammar had said, "is the longing for meeting and reunion, their fire the torment of separation."

She no longer weeps, for the tears have dried from her eyes. And she no longer goes to bake in the Sultan's kitchen; even if she wanted to, her fingers would not obey her.

She spends her days waiting, for if the night is tranquil and the stars come out, she talks to them. This star is Saïd, that one Hafez, that one Ammar, and this one Tawaddud. And that distant star there is Mahmoud. Amina speaks to each star individually, then addresses them all together. She tells them again the story from the beginning: "In the beginning, I was afraid of the sea. I was small, unformed, knowing nothing of life. I lisped when I talked, and I was afraid of nothing but the sea. I didn't know that it . . ." She tells her story without stopping, except to make sure that they are following it. "Do you hear me, Saïd?" "Isn't that what happened, Ammar?" "Don't you agree, Tawaddud?" "And you, Hafez, what do you say?" "Didn't you tell me that was what happened in Alexandria, Mahmoud?" And she goes on with the story.

Glossary
ଧୋଫ

abaya. Long outer garment, sometimes formal, that may be worn over the **jilbaab**.

abu. Literally, "father," or "father of"; also used as part of a compound name, either in addition to or instead of a man's given name—for example, "Abu Ibrahim," Father of Ibrahim.

ʿamm. Literally, "paternal uncle," but often used more loosely as a term of familiar address.

bin. Son of, as in "bin Khalid."

jilbaab. Long robelike garment worn by men; also sometimes referred to as a **jallabiyya**.

mizmar. A traditional woodwind instrument akin to the oboe, which can produce powerful and stirring music.

muezzin. Chanter who delivers the call to prayer.

riyal. Unit of currency.

rotl. A unit of weight equivalent to several kilograms.

sitt, sitti. A colloquialization of the word for "[my] lady," or "missus"; often used, especially in Egypt, to refer to or address a grandmother.

umm. Literally, "mother," or "mother of"; used in the same way as **abu** (see above), as in "Umm Ibrahim."

ୟ PROPER NAMES ଔ

Note: Each of the names listed here also exists in the standard Arabic lexicon as an ordinary noun or adjective.

Alia. Loftiness
Amina. Faithful, peaceable
Ammar. Righteous; calm, steady

Barghash. Gnat, midge
Hafez. Preserver
Khalid. Immortal
Maliha. Salty; beautiful; agreeable
Nuʿmaan. Blood
Saïd. Happy
Siraaj. Lamp, lantern
Tawaddud. Affection, flirtation

Notes

∞)(∞

CHAPTER ONE:

1. *Bismillah al-rahman al-rahim*: "in the name of God the merciful and compassionate." In Muslim societies, this is an invocation frequently uttered at the start of a task or a daily event, such as a meal; it may also be used to dispel evil spirits, particularly at times of darkness or twilight.

2. There is no god but God: *Laa ilaaha 'illa Allah*, the first part of the Muslim witness to faith, may also be used as an exclamation of surprise, awe, or consternation.

3. The Lesser Feast and the Great Feast: *Eid alFitr* and *Eid al'Adha*, respectively. The first marks the beginning of a new month (Shawwaal) in the Muslim calendar after the conclusion of Ramadan, the Islamic month of fasting; the second commemorates the sacrifice of a ram carried out by Ibrahim (Abraham), on God's releasing him from the command to sacrifice his own son.

CHAPTER TWO:

1. Here referring to African slaves, not oil, as the metaphor "black gold" commonly has it.

2. An expression used to refer to a pious person who has died.

3. "Jewel of the Arabian Sea" is a loose translation of the Arabic name, *Ghurrat-Bahr-al-Arab*, for the imaginary island that is the setting of this novel; *ghurra(t)* actually refers to the white blaze that sometimes appears on a horse's face, but it can also mean "best," "finest," or "prime."

CHAPTER THREE:

1. The tales of the mythical adventurer Sindbad, from Basra (in modern-day Iraq), of the Abbassid Caliphate, are part of the stories that make up the *One Thousand and One Nights*, told by Shahrazad (sometimes spelled "Scheherezade") to King Shahriyar. Further on in this novel is a reference to one of Sindbad's adventures in which he must defeat a demon disguised as an old man ("the old man from the sea"), who tricks Sindbad into carrying him on his shoulders, and then refuses to let go.

2. Clever Hasan (*al-shaatir Hasan*): a popular hero featured in Egyptian folk tales.

3. Orabi: an Egyptian military leader. In 1881–82 he led a revolt against the Khedive Ismail, who was in disfavor for his collusion with the Ottoman Turks; it was in the wake of this unrest that the British launched their invasion of Egypt.

4. Burg Qaitbey: *burg* means "tower," in this case the tower of Fort Qaitbey, which was erected by Sultan Qait Bey in the 1480s.

5. Burg al-Silsila: *silsila* here refers to a spit of land on the Alexandria coast, but the tower (*burg*) that must once have existed at Burg al-Silsila and given the place its name no longer stands.

6. *termis* and *chufa*: two kinds of roasted seeds sold as a snack in the streets of some Egyptian cities.

7. The reference here is to the *zaghrita*, or high-pitched ululation often uttered by women on celebratory occasions.

8. More literally, "Hey, Seymour, you with the face of a louse, who told you to act this way?" The loose translation in the text is meant to sound more like a mocking rhyme or song sung by children.

CHAPTER FIVE:

1. "The Ringdove," here somewhat adapted, is from a collection of fables known as *Kalila wa Dimna*, which originated in India about two thousand years ago. It was translated into Persian in the sixth century, and from Persian into Arabic in the eighth century.

CHAPTER EIGHT:

1. The moon is a standard metaphor applied to a beauty or an object of infatuation in Arab thought and literature.

2. The night, observed during the month of Ramadan, on which the Qur'an is said to have been revealed to the Prophet Mohammed.

CHAPTER ELEVEN:

1. ". . . daub her eyes with kohl . . .": an expression meaning, "Despite the best of intentions, you'll do her more harm than good."